A Little Too Much Is Enough

Aloha, Raegen —

my thanks,

Kathleen Tyau

3-22-2003

A Little Too Much Is Enough

by

Kathleen Tyau

FARRAR, STRAUS AND GIROUX

NEW YORK

Library of Congress catalog card number 95-060673

I am grateful to the editors and publishers who first printed my stories: "How to Cook Rice" in *Glimmer Train*, "Food for the Dead" and "Makai" (as "Island and Beyond") in *Left Bank*, "Avocado Uncle" in *American Short Fiction*, and "Moon Baby" and "All Lips" in *Story*. Thanks also to Alan Cheuse and the Syndicated Fiction Project for the National Public Radio broadcast of "Avocado Uncle."

Remembering my mother, Ruth

—how she loved

Aloha to my relatives and island friends whose lives and stories inspired me during the writing of this book and who generously gave their kokua, especially Keith Tyau, Jennifer Riley Tyau, Bryan Ching, Helen Mau, Jimmy Mau (who really did surf on an old door), William Ah Cook, Willette Ah Cook Knopp, Frank Mow, Christy Vail, Randy Hiraki, Gary Lee, and Jack Swann. I wish to acknowledge a valuable source of background information, Edward Seu Chen Mau's book, *The Mau Lineage*. Mahalo nui loa, do chiah, t'anks, eh. To those close to me, some of the persons and events in this book may seem familiar. The final banquet of characters and stories, however, results from my inclination to concoct, rather than follow, recipes. I'm grateful to the writers who gave helpful comments on my drafts without altering the seasoning. I wish I could name them all. Mahalo also to Rhea Maloney for opening the gates; Sue Austin, Barbara Dills, Candice Crossley, and Toni Kennedy for always being there; Jim Heynen, Craig Lesley, Kim Stafford (and the Northwest Writing Institute), and Rich Wandschneider for advice and support; Fishtrap for making me a Fellow; Philip Jones for good counsel; Lizzie Grossman for more than enough faith and enthusiasm; and Elisheva Urbas for fearless, gentle editing, for sharing my mind. And my love and appreciation to Paul Drews, for feeding me, believing in me, and listening to every word.

Contents

A Little Too Much Is Enough

Moon Baby

What, Mahi, you still awake? It's all your grandma's fault. Not Popo. Your tutu, Puanani, on your daddy's side, she's the one to blame. She named you after the moon, that's why you can't sleep.

I hated your name when you were small. Seem like every time she called you Mahealani, you stayed up all night long. My other babies slept real good, except for you. You cried and cried until I picked you up from the crib. I had to walk you back and forth all night. I didn't know what was making you cry. Then one night there was a full moon. I held you by the window. Ho, you fell asleep so fast.

You are a full-moon baby, that's why you can't sleep. Don't you know Mahealani means full-moon night? That's when you were born, on the night when the moon is full.

I told Kuhio they might tease you, call you mahimahi, like the fish. I fought with him, but he backed up his mother, and she won. Your tutu meant well, but she was so hard head and everybody ganged up on me. Even your popo. She said a full-moon name was good luck and I should listen to my husband's mother. Chinese style. So old-fashion. Someday when you get married, you know what I mean.

Your tutu lived with us before you were born. It was easier for me to do what she said. I fought with her only one time, when the roof leaked. She helped your grandfather put roofs on houses the time they lived on Kauai. She wanted to climb our roof and fix it during the rain. It was a hurricane! That's how hard head she was.

I wanted you to have an American first name. Suzanne Mahealani, not Mahealani Suzanne. That way you could go away to school on the mainland, and everybody could say your name right. I told her haoles can't say Mahealani. Besides, you are mostly Chinese, and this is not just Hawaii anymore. This is America.

They called you Mahi from the start. Your Uncle Joey tried to call you mahimahi, like I thought, but I put a stop to that. He said you were chunky like tuna, but you were never fat. You were strong, not soft like pure Chinese babies. Your big bones come from your daddy's side. You are like the good dark meat, the kind everybody likes. I wish I could be strong like you. And tall.

When you go to the mainland for college, you can go by your middle name. Let them call you Suzy, like the actress Suzy Wong. You have the right legs, nice and long. When you grow up, you can be a model. They pay good money for tall girls like you. You can go to New York.

But right now you are still young. You have lots of time to grow. First you need to get some sleep. Look out the window now. Do you see those clouds? Pretty soon the moon will come peeking out. Full moon tonight. Puanani was right about one thing. You are my moon baby. You are waiting for the moon.

All Lips

Nobody in my family has lips, at least not on the Chinese side. Only me, I am all lips. Lips so big I can't suck them in and breathe at the same time. Every picture of my family shows my brothers and my sister smiling, and they have no eyes, only slits, and no lips, only teeth. Just me with my eyes wide open, but you can't see them because of my eyeglasses with the iridescent blue butterfly rims, and my mouth slammed shut, so my lips don't look so big.

You can't help it, my mother says. You have your daddy's Hawaiian lips.

I wouldn't mind so much if I got the music too. If I could sing Hawaiian songs for real and not just mumble like the uncles when they're drunk. If I could dance with my knees bent low enough so I don't get whacked behind the legs by the hula teacher. If I could tell a story with my hands and shake around the island with my hips so naughty, I wouldn't mind that much. But all I got from my daddy was the lips.

Upepe lips, my brother Buzzy calls them. He even shows me the picture in *National Geographic* of the women with their chi-chis showing and the plates stuffed inside their lips. Those are Ubangi, I say, not Upepe. Close enough, he says.

So I start exercising.

Every day, when I wake up, I squeeze my lips real tight so they won't grow too big. Then I help my brother Benjie with his nose. Pinch your nose with your fingers, like this, I tell him, and then it won't stay so flat. If you want a pointy haole nose, you better do what I tell you. He doesn't know whether to believe me or not, but he is afraid to stop.

I beg the school photographer to paint away my lips. My girl friends tell me he can erase anything. What for? he asks. I don't know what for, just because. Your lips look fine, he says, but he does it anyway.

I run all the way home with my photograph. I know exactly where I want to put it. In the hall, where everybody has to pass on the way to the bathroom, the spot where my old lips hang. And I'm going to order fifty wallet-size pictures to send to my aunties and uncles and hand out to my friends.

When I get in the house, all hot and panting, I wave my picture in the air. My mother takes one look and says, Mahealani, what happened to your lips?

Nothing, I say. Aren't you going to put my picture in a frame?

Mixing Poi

My father, Kuhio, was mixing poi for the luau. Sweat ran down his arms into the stainless-steel tub full of pounded gray taro.

No worry about the sweat. Sweat makes the poi taste mo' bettah. I've been mixing poi for a long time now. First time when I was five. My mama let me. It was the luau before I got shanghaied. Some things you never forget. I didn't eat poi again until I came back from China.

As he closed his hands, the poi oozed through his thick chocolate-brown fingers, over creases and bumps.

Mixing poi is not as easy as you think. Sure, you just add a little water, then reach in and squeeze. But how much water? How long to squeeze? You have to mix it so it's just right to eat. That's why I'm doing it, because I know how. This time I'm making two-finger poi. That means not too thin and not too thick. You want the poi to stay in your mouth a little while before going down. Otherwise it's gone too quick, before you can taste.

I used to think China was just an outer island, like

Niihau, where my mama was born. She sang to me about Niihau, how she couldn't go back home. My papa was the same way. Talking all the time about China. He wanted me to go back with him, so I did. I didn't know he was going to leave me there. The whole time away, all I could think about was home. The beach, the ocean, the fish, the poi. All the things you miss when you go away. It's not easy to hold on to poi. The harder you squeeze, the more it runs away.

My father plunged his arms deeper into the poi. The taro lake rose above his elbows.

Rice, that's all they fed me. Rice and salt fish, rice and pickled cabbage. We ate a little bit of fish and a big bowl of rice to fill us up. I still love my rice, but, oh, I missed my poi like you don't know how. I asked my popo in China, When is my papa coming back for me? I talked to her half in hakka, half in sign language. I scraped my two fingers in my bowl and put them in my mouth. She gave me another scoop of rice.

He shook his head and stopped mixing. The poi swallowed his arms like quicksand.

Poi is very hard head. Sticks to your hands, sticks to your mouth, hard to wash off. But taste real ono with kalua pig and lomi lomi salmon. All the salty food. Poi is like staying home. You get tired if you eat out too much. When I came back to the islands, I couldn't eat enough. Where is my poi? I asked my mama. Where is my squid, my mango, my breadfruit? I ate up everything before they could take it away. Sure, I love my rice. But poi is what I was hungry for.

My father's arms rose out of the vat. The poi fell off his muscles like sheets of gray rain. He scraped the poi down his left arm, off his palm, off each finger, one by one. He did the same with his right arm, then reached for a bowl.

You have to hold it in your hand like a baby. Lift it up easy, squeeze, then twist. See how the poi stops falling for a while? That's when you stick the bowl underneath. That's all the time you have, so you better be quick, just one second before it falls.

Poi Knuckles, Rice Feet

Rice mouth yells at the neighbor boy who rides his bike across the lawn. You better stop that. My brother going give you lickings if you don't watch out. Rice mouth doesn't know how to shut up and eat, shut up and act like a lady, sweet.

Poi knuckles reach for the hard green mangoes on the lowest branch. Okay, man, you asked for it. Poi arm winds up, gives the boy a good bean on the okole. Boy falls off his bike and cries.

Rice feet turn around and run like hell before the boy's mother comes out and yells. Run barefoot up the gravel driveway, quick inside the house and up the stairs.

Poi brain remembers too late the baby Nani sleeping in her crib. Going get lickings if I wake the baby up. Supposed to watch her while Mama's at the store.

Rice hands play Brahms' Lullaby for the crying baby Nani. One finger each hand, count the notes, hunt for the keys, hit them one by one. Lullaby, don't you cry, but the baby shrieks. What, you like me play something fast? Bang the keys hard, head bobs up and down, smile, big Liberace smile. Play real loud, louder than the baby can scream. Okay, okay, okay, give up. Stop. Pick the baby Nani up. Whatsamatta you? Poke the little nose, not too hard. Why you no like good kind music? Rock the baby back and forth.

Poi fingers play again soft, *aloha oe,* with the eyes shut tight and the mouth wide open, *aloha oe,* and the baby Nani cooing while the body sways like the aunties dancing, like the uncles playing their ukuleles and guitars at night.

Watch My Hands

Tutu Puanani teaches me the hula. She ties a scarf around her muumuu so I can see her okole sway.

Hapa haole hula, she says. They like you watch the okole, but you better watch the hands. See how I make my hands go like this along my body? See how I go up over the hill and down into the valley? And then out. Way, way out, all the way to the ocean. Now watch my okole. See my hips, how I move. Sassy little wahine. See how I shake around the island. Not so fast, take your time. Got a long way around and everybody watching. But you scold them. No, no! Keep your eyes on the hands. Then you give them a wink. That's right. Naughty hula hands. See how they go up to my breast. Has to be the left one, because this is my heart. My pu'uwai. That's where my love is. See how I roll my hands over and over like the surf. I wrap my pu'uwai like a gift. And now I open up my hands. See them go all the way to shore. Giving you my love. Aloha no.

My tutu was born on the island of Niihau. Her family

lived in the town of Pu'uwai. Their house, the land, all belonged to the Robinson family.

Those days you cannot just come and go anytime you please. If you like go away, you can, but that's it. Pau. No can go back. Maybe you will be wanting too much. My family is very happy on Niihau. They grow the best garden on the island. My makuakane, my papa, and my brothers, they catch the most fish. Plenty lobster too, back in those days. I help my mama make poi, pick opihi and seaweed and pupu shell. We make the most beautiful lei in all Hawaii nei. Pupu o Niihau. But me, I have a mind of my own. Talk back, no listen, think too much. I took the mail boat to Kauai when I was sixteen. My mama, my papa, everybody cry when I go, but not me. I never cry. I never look back. Soon as the boat go, I am standing right in front.

See my fingers, how they touch like I am praying. My fingers touch, but not the palms. This is my hale. This is my home. See how I open the hands. This is my hale, and I am leaving. Going by boat. See the ocean waves. Saying goodbye. See the fish, how they swim. See the rain. Watch it fall.

On Kauai my tutu went to work for the wife of the sugar plantation boss.

Haole lady, but real good to me. She teach me how to speak English, how to write my name, how to believe in Jesus. I take care the babies, clean the house, wash clothes. I do anything she like. Your grandpa, first time he see me, I am washing clothes. He say, Do mine. I tell him, Do it yourself, what you think I am? I pay you, he say. Sorry, I shake my head. I only wash clothes for the boss lady and for my kane. Okay, he say. I marry you.

This is my heart. I go by sea to the one I love. See how I raise my hands high in the sky, then open. Falling, like rain. I am still young. Going around the island. Sassy little wahine. Giving my pu'uwai. Finding my home.

Tutu strings plumeria one by one with a long needle and cotton thread. She makes a lei for me to wear while I am dancing the hula.

See this flower? No good. Good, good, no good. See the brown on the edge? See the wrinkle in the skin? Flowers like that already too old.

She throws the unwanted plumeria over the rock wall into the drainage canal behind our house. The flowers float away quickly in the rushing water.

———

My popo, Choy Kim How, puffs rice in the wok for toong mai, my favorite cookie. She talks to me in hakka so I can learn to cook and speak Chinese at the same time. She pours hot syrup over the rice and stirs the sticky rice with a wooden spoon.

See the rice, like family, always sticking together. Now I'm going to pour the rice into the basket before it gets too hard. Watch my hands while I talk, so you know what I am saying.

I came by boat, but I was not a picture bride. Before I was born, my family knew who my husband was. Your goong goong's great-uncle's wife was my goong goong's cousin. Far enough apart, yet close enough to keep the family tie. Fook was an island boy, born in Honolulu. I didn't meet him until we got married. He came all the way to China to get me.

Popo spreads the rice quickly with an oiled rolling pin.

You have to work fast. Don't stay in one place too long. When the rice is cool, cut it with the cleaver. See how many diamonds you can cut.

Jagged pieces of rice fall away as Popo lifts the diamond-shaped bars out of the basket. She puts the good pieces in big tin cans and leaves the scraps for me to eat. They are still warm, smelling of peanuts and oil and melted sugar. She gives the odd shapes names, first in hakka, then in English. Makes me repeat them after her. Abb—duck. Mao—hat. Goon—stick. Hok—crane.

We were married in your goong goong's family village in Chungshan. When we left for the islands, I said goodbye to my family once and for all. I belonged to your goong goong and his parents now. Fook was very brown and had big muscles when he came for me. From swimming in the ocean, he said. So much ocean you cannot imagine. Even more than you have in China. His mother gave me jade. Fook gave me a rock. From the volcano, he said. All the volcano you want.

Popo opens her teak jewelry chest and brings out a crumbling chunk of black lava. She presses it to my cheek.

Goo nei hei ngar sak. Ngar siau dor. This is my rock. My little island. See how perfectly it fits into my palm.

Food for the Dead

Gold and silver paper money burns next to bowls of sun-warmed dumplings. We have come to the cemetery with my grandmother to bai san, to pray for our dead grandfather and bring him food, whiskey, and money. Popo lights red candles with the smoking punk. Last night we folded many pieces of paper money, which Popo sends to Goong Goong by fire so he will have lots of money to buy houses and clothes in heaven. She wails softly in a singsong voice and presses her palms together and bows toward the grave. I crawl into the circle of her arms and bow with her hands covering mine. Three times I bow, and then my cousins take their turns. I play around the gravesite while the others pray.

Don't step on Goong Goong's head. If you step on his head, he will think you do not honor him.

I tiptoe around the concrete border of the grave, careful not to touch the grass, holding my breath and crossing my fingers when I slip.

Mama, tell me about Goong Goong.

Your goong goong was the only one who could stop you from crying at the table. You kicked and screamed so much he tied your feet to the high chair. He gave you funny face and made you laugh. He looked like a beach boy. He lifted weights and loved to surf. He owned a store in Waikiki and used the money to buy land. If he had lived long enough, we would be rich. You would be rich. But he got sick all of a sudden. He had a bad cough. The doctors thought he had pneumonia, but two months later he died of lung cancer. And you wouldn't stop crying. You cried so much I had to stay home from his funeral. So don't step on Goong Goong's head. We'll go home soon and you can eat.

We pour the whiskey and tea on the grass and carry the bowls of food to the car. Back at home, Popo warms up the noodles and dumplings and everyone sits down at the long table to eat. But I cannot. Everything feels lumpy. I close my eyes and try to remember my goong goong laughing, carrying me on his shoulders as he runs along the beach. I am hanging on to his head, holding on tight, trying not to fall.

Digging a Hole to China

Watch me, Sis, and dig like this. Gotta make the hole big enough, but not that big. Just big enough for you and me. Benjie can't go; he's too small. We only going stay little while, not too long, just long enough to say hello, then come back home and sleep. You know how to say hello in Chinese? Ngee how mah, that's what Popo said. Say it. Ngee how mah. That's good enough. We only going stay little while, so the hole don't need to be that big, and you don't have to say that much.

We'll dig the hole so it comes out by our cousin's house in China. I know where they live. I heard Uncle Danny them talking. Hong Kong, that's where they went, so that's where we go too. Lots of people go Hong Kong, so must not be that hard to find. But first we gotta dig the hole so don't stop yet. Gotta make it big enough, just right for you and me. Too late to go today, but tomorrow we go for sure. We dig the hole, go home eat, and then I gotta take out the garbage. But after breakfast we go. Better pack lunch. Not too much. We not going stay that long, just long enough to say hello. Why don't you pack some rice ball, guava juice, two can Vienna Sausage. Take the juice from the freezer. That way the juice stay cold.

Dig the hole slant like this so the dirt don't fall back inside. See how I dig? No need to make it that big, just big enough. Only going stay little while. Can you say it? Ngee how mah. That means how are you. If you get hungry, say yak fan, but better not say it, I hear them guys starving. That's why we gotta pack lunch, go, and come back quick.

Maybe we can bring back our cousin. The one Aunty Ah Oi said look just like me. I forget his name, Wah something. Have to ask Aunty to tell me again. She said we could pass for brothers. So when we reach Hong Kong, we just look for the boy who look like me. And then we bring him back if he like come. Just to visit. He can sleep in our room, on my bed. I can sleep on the floor. He can go school with us and sit by me. And we can make him fried rice for breakfast. Portuguese sausage too. And Spam. Bet you cannot get Spam in Hong Kong.

Put the food inside your Mickey Mouse lunch box. That way the lunch stay cold. No need crackseed. Lolo, that's where they make crackseed for the whole wide world. When we get there, you can have any kind seed you want. I wonder if he really look like me. I can let him ride my bike. We can take turns sleeping on the floor. He can teach me how to speak Chinese. I can show him how to bodysurf.

Gotta dig fast if we going tomorrow. Make the hole slant so we can slide all the way, get there fast. But we only going stay little while. Not overnight, because them guys starving. Uncle said he send money to China every time. I wish I could remember the name. Gotta ask Aunty. She said they never write back. She only saw him one time, but she said could be my brother. Some guys might think he was me.

Which You Rather Have

Which you rather have, wind for the rest of your life or sunshine all the time? my brother Benjie asks. We are lying on our backs in the middle of the schoolyard looking for animal clouds and playing our favorite game. He asks first, so I must choose. But first, I need to ask him questions.

Will I be able to stop the wind whenever I want?

No, wind just blows all the time.

Will it blow so strong I can go up the Pali and jump off the cliff without falling down?

Oh no, it just blows any kind way. Sometime strong, sometime junk. Cannot make up its mind.

Then what about the sun? Will I be able to play in the sun all day and not get brown?

Sure, man, you can play all you want.

And will the sun stay up and never go down?

Yeah, and you won't get sleepy, and you can stay up late and play outside all night long.

I already know what my answer is. He forces the sun on me because he wants to keep what's left. I know, because

I am more than just his older sister who taught him this game. We have pricked our fingers and traded blood, new blood, not the kind we had before we were born but the kind that belongs to only us. And that's how come he wants the wind. He wants what I want.

When we go up to the Pali and stop the car at the lookout point, I lean as far forward as I can into the wind. I like the way the wind blows up my muumuu. It makes me feel like a balloon going up. I dream about going to the Pali to hide when the dive bombers attack Pearl Harbor and when the tidal wave comes. The wind at the Pali makes me feel strong.

But when we go over the Pali to our cousins' house, I have to hold Benjie's hand. He's too big to sit in the front with our parents, so he stays in the back with me. We roll the windows up tight and lean toward the cliff so we can't fall off.

Don't worry, I tell him, you're not going to fall, but he still clings to me. So I say, But you better watch out for the Obake. Or Pele. He looks at me, waiting for me to go on. I look straight ahead. I don't know who's up here right now, I say, but never mind, Pele or the Obake can come get you. If they want. He shuts his eyes real tight and pretends he doesn't hear. Okay, which you rather have come get you, Pele or the Obake? He is so scared he cannot ask the questions I am waiting for. Come on, you have to choose or it's bad luck. You want Pele to come get you? She's very beautiful and she likes little boys. She has big red lips and hair all the way down to her ankles, and she sings to you the whole time. Makes you fall asleep. My voice drops down real low. Or maybe you rather have the Obake? She has no eyes, no mouth, not even a nose, only a flat white face. He looks at me with big eyes. But still he says nothing. So I say, You rather have Pele come and take you to the volcano and throw you in? Your ashes will fly all the way up to the clouds. I can see him start to think. Or the Obake can come get you. She can steal you from the car. She knows how to stop the car, you know. She knows how to break the lock. He's looking at me now.

Not, he says. Not.

I'm talking real slow now, and I'm looking at him like I mean it. The Obake cannot talk, I say. No mouth. No lips. No eyes. She just waits for you to get so scared you die.

Pele, Pele! he screams. I want Pele!

Fine, I say, then I'll take the Obake. She'll teach me how to change my face into anything I want. I can make myself look like Roy Rogers or Bozo the Clown or even Santa Claus. And I can ride a reindeer or a horse, and I can juggle uku-billion beanbags at one time.

Then I want to have the Obake, he cries, and I'm going to be the Lone Ranger, and I'm going to get Pele and the Obake and I'm going to kill them dead. He sits up straight in the car seat now, and his eyes are like bowling balls getting ready to roll. Pow! Pow! He lets go of my hand.

How to Cook Rice

Cook rice the way I show you and it will always turn out. Watch how I do it. This is the best way.

Did you wash your hands? And pin back your hair so it doesn't get in your eyes. Wash two cups, three if we're having salty fish for supper, four if we're having company. Buy the best rice in big sacks. Hinode is the best. Wash it good, like this, so the talcum powder comes off. You don't want to eat what we put on the baby. Just swirl the rice good with your hands, like this. See how white the water gets? Pin your hair back, Sister, so it doesn't get in your eyes. Take Daddy his slippers and give him a kiss when he gets home from work. Rinse the rice until the water is clear. Save the rinsewater for the orchids. And pick out all the rocks and bugs.

Save your papaya seeds too. Dig a hole in the ground like this and stick them in. Water them every day and soon you will have a papaya tree and all your papayas will be sweet and you can have as many as you want. Eat a papaya every morning and it will keep you regular. Wear bright colors. Red is good.

Kiss Daddy every day when he gets home from work and he will love you. Let him talk and just don't listen if it bothers you. Water your orchids every day. Your daddy was shanghaied, so he can't help it if he talks. Black and white are colors of the dead, so wear bright colors. Red is a good color for you. Water your orchids every day and plant your papaya seeds just like I showed you.

Cover the rice with water and put your middle finger in the pot, like this. See the water come up just to the first joint of your finger? No matter what size your pot is or how far you are from home, use your joint to measure and your rice will always turn out right.

Pin your hair back, Mahealani. How many times do I have to tell you? This is why I want you to wear your hair short, so it doesn't get in your way. Long hair is for loose women, so short is always better. Don't sit in a boy's lap. And don't let him touch your personal. Wash your personal good so you don't smell bad. Did you wash your hands?

Wear old clothes to the dentist, so we don't have to pay his bill right away. We can shop for new clothes for school while your brothers are at the dentist. Don't wear black and white. Buy bright colors—red is good. Hide the new clothes in the car trunk so Dr. Chun won't see them or he'll make me pay up today. Go, hide now, and don't let your daddy see them.

After the water boils down, cover the pot. Pretend you are listening. Turn the heat down. Just don't listen if he bothers you. Let the rice simmer until it's done.

Always wear clean panties, pretty things. A woman

always wants to feel good underneath. You can wear leopardskin, polka dot, lace, anything. Just look like a lady on top and walk like this. Pin your hair back, Sister.

Black and white are for the dead, just like chrysanthemums. April is the month of the dead. That's when I was born—in the month of the dead, on Bad Luck Friday, Friday the 13th. We must go to the graveyards in April and bai san for Popo and Goong Goong in heaven. I hate to go, but we must. Kneel and bow your head like this and make your hands go up and down like this. Three times is good enough. Don't eat the food on the grave. That's for Popo and Goong Goong to eat. And don't walk on their heads. Did you wash your hands? And don't give me chrysanthemums for my birthday.

Water your orchids every day. Wash your personal. Wear red dresses. Plant your papaya seeds. Buy the best rice. Wash it good.

Don't think about things that make you sad and they will go away. Save your money, even if it's only a quarter a day. By Christmas you will have enough to buy something good. You can buy a red dress. Wear lace panties. Hide them. Don't sit on a boy's lap. When you go away to school, I'll send you orchids and panties.

Save the rinsewater for the orchids. Pretend you are listening. Hide. Pin your hair back, Sister. Cook your rice this way and it will always turn out right.

Still the Same Saimin

Eat saimin with your uncles and aunties and cousins in the restaurant after the football game. Extra-large bowls for the uncles, medium bowls for the aunties, and small bowls for the kids. Remove the wooden chopsticks from their paper wrapping and rub them together fast to make the splinters go away. Rub to make sparks. Rub to make fire for the cave. Enough, enough rubbing, stop playing with your chopsticks and sit up straight. Use your chopsticks to rub shoyu and mustard in a small dish. Watch how the uncles rub. Smooth circles, slow at first, not too much mustard, not so fast. Rub until the steaming bowls come out of the kitchen. Rub until your bowl sits down in front.

Play with the long, skinny noodles, too long for one bite. Smell the broth, feel it sting like the fumes of Mama's home permanent. Count the slices of char siu floating on top, take small bites to make the meat last longer. Chase the chopped green onions with your big white spoon. Too hot, so blow before you eat. Scoop from the edge first. Let

the noodles rest a little while in your spoon. Still too hot.
Drink your ice water. Eat, don't talk.

———

Eat saimin at the state fair. Hand the lady in the booth
your paper scrip, three tickets for one bowl. Take the chopsticks only. Don't need a spoon, just drink straight from the
bowl. Hold the bowl up high so people can see you and
don't bump. Walk very slowly to the picnic table by the
Ferris wheel. Pay attention, don't watch the Ferris wheel
go up and down. Stand on the table to see how tall the
noodles get. Raise the chopsticks way up and up, like Jack
and the Beanstalk, up to the sky. Let the wicked witch blow
the saimin cool. Whack, Okay, sit down, where's your
spoon? Put your head close to the bowl, eat fast now.

———

Eat saimin after going to the movies with the gang.
Eye up Jimmy, Kono, and Chow, so cool, so tough in duck-
tails, bell-bottoms, shirts tight at the waist. Watch them
shuffle into the all-night saimin stand, slap-slap with their
slippers on the concrete floor. Listen to them order. One
big bowl saimin. One nada one, just like him, and don't
forget da kim chee. The waitress doesn't crack one smile,
no personality. She slings her needle hips to one side, snaps
her gum loud. Behind her a rattling fan, the night boy mop-
ping the floor with Spic and Span. Stick a quarter in the
jukebox, man. Rock to Elvis, hold the chopsticks close and
sing. Oooo, oooo da hot. Blow on it, Chow. Noodles shake
from booth to booth, barely touch lips, turn the dark night
chili-pepper hot.

———

Eat saimin after cruising Waikiki, checking out the guys, the coeds, their bikinis too small, their breasts so big, their skin turning red. Hot and tired and hungry now, cross Kalakaua Avenue and head for McDonald's. See the carefully weighed noodles and soup waiting in Styrofoam bowls next to the teriyaki burgers. Stand in line. Order a large Coke and a big bowl of saimin. One size only, not enough, but you can always come back for more. Grab some plastic packets of shoyu and mustard, wooden chopsticks wrapped in white paper. Sit at the picnic table under the gazebo next to the beach. Eat the saimin, still the same, the noodles long and wrinkled, the hot broth bringing tears to your eyes. Blow, don't think. Watch the old men play cards while you eat.

Pupus and Uncles

Until the aunties drag them home, the uncles eat pupus, drink beer, and play cards on the lanai. They play trumps and poker and what-the-hell. They eat dried cuttlefish, squid warmed on the burner of the electric stove, boiled octopus, and tripe. Salty, hot food that makes them reach for more beer. Stink and tough, a man's kind of food.

Brown rainwater rushes by in the drainage canal behind the house. Mosquitoes hide from the cloud of cigarettes and smoking green coils of mosquito punk. The aunties rock the babies in the living room. The older children run in and out of the house, yelling and laughing and slamming the screen door.

The uncles squat on metal chairs around folding card tables. They sit as if holding drums between their legs. They wear what uncles wear for poker—thin, yellowing under-shirts stretched over their bellies and faded aloha shirts un-buttoned, baggie Bermuda shorts, Japanese rubber slippers. The uncles are whole or part Chinese, Japanese, Portuguese, Hawaiian. They are brothers, cousins, friends of the family.

They work for the military—welding on the battleships at Pearl Harbor, maintaining the barracks at Scofield, servicing the cargo planes at Hickam airfield. They lift and drill and hammer all day. At night they play cards, eat, drink, tell jokes, talk story.

Uncle Wing sucks loudly from his can of beer, then burps. He pats his stomach, then throws down a card. "You watch me beat 'em," he says, grinning at his young niece sitting next to him.

"I never tell you guys da one about da Japanee guy?" he asks. "Who made da illegal left turn?"

The uncles grunt, chew, follow suit.

"Da policeman, big Hawaiian guy, he says, 'Aay, brah, you never see da kine sign on da road? Say NO LEFT TURN. So why you went turn, hah?' "

The uncles drink, rearrange their cards.

" 'Hai,' say da Japanee guy." Uncle Wing bows several times from the waist. " 'Sure I follow da sign. It say, TURN LEFT, NO?' "

The uncles laugh, shake their heads. Uncle Wing slaps a card down hard on the table.

"Trumps! I win," he says. "Easy come, easy go." He turns to his niece. "See what I told you. You my lucky charm."

The uncles groan, toss their cards on the table, scrape back chairs, shuffle across the concrete. Time for more beer and pupus.

Uncle Joey's Squab

Uncle Joey turns the bird on a grill made out of a coffee can and chicken wire. I crouch beside him in the driveway of Popo's house. He doesn't like to babysit, but Popo makes him. He blows on the charcoal until it glows red. The bird's drumsticks are the same size as my uncle's knuckles.

"How can you eat that bird?" I ask him.

"Easy, with my mouth. And it's a squab, not a bird. I let you try some. Taste real ono. Better than chicken any day."

I shake my head. Not supposed to play with fire. Not sure I want to eat a bird, even if it is a squab. At least he didn't hang it from the clothesline like my father does with the chickens. Didn't slit the throat and let it squawk and jerk, didn't let the blood fly all over the yard.

"You watch it for me," he says, "while I go inside the house and get some shoyu. Don't let it burn now. Here, just turn it like this so it doesn't get stuck to the grill. It won't bite you. See, it's almost done. Nice big one, eh?

Can't buy this kind. Watch it now. I'll be right back. And don't let Fat Alfred get it.''

Fat Alfred lives across the street. Nobody knows for sure how old he is. They say he flunked third grade four times. He's as big as my uncle, but not as smart. But smart enough to wait until my uncle goes inside before coming across the street to bother me.

Alfred sticks his stomach in my face. His T-shirt doesn't cover his belly button. I try to keep my eyes on the bird. Try not to look at Alfred's big, stink toes hanging over the edge of his dirty rubber slippers.

"Aay, teetah, what you cooking? Sure smell ono." He's trying to be nice, because he wants to eat.

"Squab. You better go way."

"Squab? Man, where you get da kine squab?"

"My uncle went catch um."

"Wow, big one, man. Aay, that look just like da kine pigeon my friend Wayne go raise. You know, he's missing one."

Alfred squats beside me to take a closer look.

"Hey, I bet that's the one. Oh, man, I going tell him your Uncle Joey went shoot um. You guys going be in big trouble. Big trouble, man."

I grab the bird and run behind the ti leaf plants, where I have stashed a pile of green mangoes.

"Aay, no make li' dat," shouts Alfred. "No make li' dat, I told you. Aay, no throw the mango. You like beef or what? You like I break your face?"

He ducks again and again, and then I'm out of mangoes and Alfred starts throwing rocks. One nicks my ear. I scream. The kitchen door slams and Uncle Joey comes running out.

"Hey, what's going on? Alfred, why you stay picking on her? She just one kid, man. Why don't you pick on somebody your own size?" Uncle Joey grabs a rock and winds up, but Alfred hides behind my grandfather's Ford.

"You like I knock you on the side of the head or what?" My uncle yells, but he doesn't throw. He knows he better not ding the car. "I take you down by the stream and give you lickings you never forget. So you better go hide. I'm telling you, man. Don't say I never give you warning."

Alfred runs back to his garage. Uncle Joey throws a rock at Alfred's bike lying on the lawn, another one at the mailbox, but Alfred doesn't come out. Uncle Joey turns to me. I'm still hiding behind the ti leaves.

"Mahi," he shouts. "Where's the squab?"

I come out holding my ear with one hand. I hand him the bird with the other. I am holding it by the ankles.

"How come it's all covered with dirt?"

"I was hiding it."

"Why?"

"He said you went steal it." Crying now, still holding my ear. "He said it's Wayne's pigeon."

"I didn't steal it! And this ain't pigeon, man. This is squab. That's—that's a wild kind of pigeon. It was just flying around when I was practice-shooting with my BB gun. So who's your friend, me or Fat Alfred?"

He holds out the front of his T-shirt so I can blow.

"Did he hurt you? Did he get you?"

Shake my head no. "Almost."

"What a coward. Picking on kids. You saw how he went back inside the house. He was scared, man. So how many mangoes did you hit him with?"

"Five."

"Five? Ha! No wonder he was mad. Good thing you had the stash. What I told you? Man, I wish I could have seen it."

He blows at the dusty, half-roasted bird. Picks out bits of gravel.

"I tell you what. I can wash it off. Yeah, I'll just rinse it off with the hose, rub on some oil, throw it back on the grill. Nobody can tell the difference once we put the shoyu on. Quick, go inside the house and get some oil. And don't tell Popo or we're really gonna be in trouble. Just tell her I need the oil for something, but don't tell her it's for the squab, and don't say BB gun. Tell her it's for the lawn mower and I ran out of the other kind oil. Yeah, tell her I'm going to mow the lawn. Well, what you waiting for? This squab is going to be real ono."

Oregon Lap Ap

After I showed him the fourth photograph of ducks, ducks floating in a mountain lake near Mt. Hood, Uncle Wing said, Next time you come home, why don't you bring me a duck?

You get plenty duck in Oregon. I know, I seen the picture. Bring me one nice juicy one, not too old. The old one is tough. Bring me one duck and I show you how for make lap ap. Real good for eat, lap ap. Cost plenty money too. I saw one whole store of lap ap the time Uncle Sukey and me went San Francisco Chinatown. He told me, Wing, look all the duck, look all the lap ap hanging by the neck. Make me so ono just to think. I brought home three. Couldn't fit more in the suitcase. And lap ap not cheap, you know.

You get so much duck in Oregon, why don't you go into business? All you need is some Hawaiian salt and a blower. You can dry the duck out in the shed. Got no blower? Use your hair dryer. Same thing. Make sure the air not too hot, that's all.

You bring me one duck and I show you how. No, maybe you better bring two or three. Just in case the first one don't turn out. Maybe I can get a recipe from my friend the cook at the Golden Rooster. I should have asked the owner of the shop in San Francisco. But why should he tell me? Business could go bust.

Make sure the duck is alive. Otherwise you don't know if it's fresh. Gotta have fresh duck for lap ap or people can tell. Just by the smell. Old duck don't smell right. Just put the duck in a box. Punch a few holes. Make sure you feed it before the plane ride. Dead duck is no good. No, wait, gotta go through quarantine. Two weeks, long time. Too long. Tough luck. Guess you gotta kill it first. Then you can pack it in dry ice.

No worry, duck is easy for kill. Just like chicken. Hang it on the clothesline. Slit it by the throat, right here, and not too close to the house. Let the blood drain out. Put it in boiling water to make the feathers loose. Real easy, I tell you. Don't shake your head no.

Bag of Mango

Take this bag of mango when we go to visit Aunty Nona. I saved some for you to eat, but we have to take some to Nona because she doesn't have this kind. This is Hayden mango. Real sweet, just like the kind we used to pick at Popo's house. The tree Buzzy used to climb. The one you fell off.

Nona loves mango, especially Hayden. So does Lucy. My sisters, they sure love to eat. Last time Lucy came from the mainland, she ate a whole bag of mango all by herself. The boy next door gave them to me. We had mango up to here. Seems like everybody gives us mango. I just get rid of one bag and another one shows up. I was going to take the mango over to Nona's house, but Lucy came over and she ate one mango, and then another one, and before you know it, the whole bag was gone. Lucy can't get good mango in California. Not this kind anyway.

I hate to always give mango to Nona. She can hardly fit her clothes. She's always wearing tent dress, tent dress. She says it's the style, but she's just too fat. And Lucy comes home only every once in a while. But that's okay. I send her mango bread. I just cut up the mango and freeze it. Then at Christmas time I make mango bread to send to her and all our friends and family on the mainland. To you and Lucy and to your college friend, the family in Bend who invited you for Thanksgiving, and the nice lady who helped you open up your bank account. I forget her name, Grace somebody. Next time you see her, tell her hi for me. She always sends me a Christmas card and a nice thank-you note.

Everybody always wants my recipe. I'm not chang; I give it to them. But their mango bread never turns out like mine. Not as moist. That's because the original recipe calls for one cup of mango, but I use two cups, sometimes three. It all depends on how many mangoes I have to get rid of.

You don't have to eat all the mango bread I send you. Just freeze it, or give some to your neighbor across the fence, the one who gave me tomatoes when I came to visit. The next time I get a bag of mango, I'll bake mango bread and send some to you even though it's not Christmas.

Too bad I can't send you fresh mango. But you can take it home frozen if you cut it up and take out the seed. Can't take the seed, because it might have bugs. In fact, you can take this whole bag of mango home. I'll slice them up for you. I can give mango to Nona the next time somebody gives me some.

A Little
Too Much
Is Enough

All day long I starved myself, but before we left for the wedding I sat at the kitchen table and watched my father eat saimin. I sat so close to him the steam from the hot broth made my eyes water.

"Get a bowl," he said.

I shook my head. I was determined to save my stomach for dinner that night. I knew the food would be good. My cousin Beetle Wong was getting married, and his parents were relieved that he was marrying Chinese. And not just any old Chinese. Beetle had met Teena Lum-Tong while cruising Kahala Mall, where the rich girls shop. Three hundred fifty relatives and friends were celebrating at a Chinese nine-course dinner in Waikiki after the wedding.

My father says the noodles sop up the alcohol and keep him from getting drunk. When my mother said, "Better eat another bowl of saimin, Kuhio," I knew they were preparing for a long night of drinking with the uncles.

———

At the entrance to the Hilton banquet hall I checked the guest list for my name. When I discovered I was sitting with the older cousins, I nearly cartwheeled across the room. At fourteen I had finally graduated from the children's table.

The oldest one at my table was Frankel Choy, a cousin from my mother's side. And his wife, Wei Ling, six months hapai. My brother Buzzy. The twins, Sue-Sue and Sam. My cousin Rhoda Chew, who everybody calls Tookie. Tookie was two years older than me so I always got stuck wearing her hand-me-downs. Finally I came to his name. Robert Michelangelo Wong. My second cousin Bobby. Nobody told me he was coming home. Our fathers were cousins, which meant we saw each other only at big parties now, at funerals or weddings.

Bobby wasn't tough to spot in the crowded room. He played guard for Oregon State on a basketball scholarship. Even sitting, he was a grasshopper in a swarm of ants. All legs.

I forced myself not to run to the table. I pulled out my chair like it was my mother's good china. Buzzy was already there, trading elephant jokes with Sue-Sue and Sam. I ignored him. Pretended I didn't see Bobby at first.

"Hi, Frankel," I said. "Hi, Wei Ling. Is the baby kicking yet?" I pointed at her stomach, which still looked smaller than mine. Not waiting for an answer, I turned to Bobby. "Aay, Bobby, howzit? Teaching them haoles how to play ball?"

Bobby greeted me by standing up, unlike the other boy cousins, who slouched deeper in their chairs. I liked the way he had to look down at me.

"Hey, Mahealani," he said softly. "How you doing,

kid? Long time no see." He leaned over and squeezed my shoulder. I reached up for his hand. Too late. Wished I could say hello all over again, cut the pidgin, call him Robert Michelangelo, like I wrote in my diary.

Even though we were five years apart in age, Bobby and I always ended up playing together when our families met for picnics and potluck suppers back when we were kids. We played kickball, sky inning, doctor and nurse. The day I told him I was never getting married, he let me be the doctor. Let me feel his forehead, take his pulse, perform the operation that saved his life. Then one day, while we were playing in the empty lot next to the sugar-cane fields, I saw Bobby make shi-shi behind a boulder. I only saw him from the back, and I didn't see anything, because he kept his pants on, but my legs felt weak. When he came back to play with me, he threw me a sky ball and said, "Try catch this one." But I let the ball fall behind the keawe bushes and spent a long time crawling around in the dirt pretending I was looking for it.

I don't know how Tookie managed to get the seat next to Bobby. She must have switched her placecard with mine so she could moon all over him. I never should have told her how I felt about him. Once she knew, she didn't stop plotting.

"I'm going to Oregon State too," she had said. "Bobby will still be around when I get there."

"Forget it, Rhoda." She hated when I called her that. "You'll never pass the test." But deep down inside I was worried. I had to get to Oregon before she did.

She wore too much mascara that evening and her lipstick was smeared, but of course I didn't tell her. I couldn't keep my eyes off her dress. It was a body-hugging cheongsam with a long slit up the side, her mother's dress, and it was red, like mine, except that my dress had a loose, dropped waist, so I could eat without having to suck in my stomach. I knew everyone would look at her and then at me and then back at her again. At least her dress was too big in the bust and too tight in the hips, so the wrong parts of Tookie showed.

I decided to play it cool. Bobby had once said to me, "The thing I like about you, Mahi, is you aren't silly." Tookie talked too much and snorted like a baby pig when she laughed. I figured she would drive Bobby nuts after a while, and when the band started playing, he'd come to me to escape. I took my place between the twins, Sue-Sue and Sam.

Then Uncle Joey came over and made one of the twins switch tables with him. The aunties and uncles called Joey "Small Uncle" because he was the youngest, not because of his size. Next to him, everyone else in the family looked like termites.

"That's right," said Uncle Wing. "Go and sit with the kids. More food for us." The aunties laughed. Buzzy and I and the cousins at my table groaned. Nobody wanted Uncle Joey at their table, because he dug around for the best pieces of meat and messed up the serving dish. Then he ate so fast everyone at his table had to eat faster to keep up.

"No, no, go back," said Tookie, but it was too late.

"I think I'll go help out the kids too," said Aunty Nona, making her way to our table.

"Oh no. That's all we need," I said. "Why do we have to get stuck with both of them?"

"Shhh, they'll hear you," said Wei Ling, who clearly was not related to any of us.

The other twin moved to the table with the big eaters,

which left me with Uncle Joey on one side and Aunty Nona on the other. My father said Aunty Nona was bossy because she should have been a teacher but sold crackseed instead. But my mother disagreed. She said, "Nona means well. She has a good heart. She just loves to eat."

That night, as Aunty Nona sat down next to me, I prayed I wasn't the one at the table she was goodhearted enough to boss. She looked like a Christmas gift in her long white muumuu with the big red hibiscus print. She grinned at me.

"How lucky," she said. "I get to sit by my favorite niece."

"Oh, Aunty," I said, trying not to wince as she pinched my arm. "I'm so glad you came to sit with us." I didn't want Bobby to think I was a whiner.

———

Uncle Joey banged his water glass with a spoon, signaling for a toast. I poured tea in my cup and wondered how I could get someone to slip me some Scotch. Uncle Joey raised his jigger in the direction of the newlyweds, Beetle and Teena.

"Here's to you two," he said. "If you two no love we too as much as we love you two, then here's to we all."

He had borrowed that toast from somebody else's wedding, but I loved it anyway. I could repeat it in my sleep, because he gave the same toast at every family wedding. Sometimes I lay awake at night trying to figure out where the t-o's and t-o-o's and t-w-o's belonged. I asked him once, but he looked worried that I might steal his lines.

We knocked our glasses together, Beetle kissed Teena,

Frankel kissed Wei Ling's baby finger, and Tookie and I sighed at the same time. Aunty Hannah Mele sang the blessing in Hawaiian, and finally, eons after my father's bowls of saimin, out came the food.

The waiters marched into the hall carrying enormous platters of cold steamed chicken covered with chopped ginger, green onions, oil, and sprigs of Chinese parsley. Everyone clapped and started eating. Except for our table.

"Wait," said Aunty Nona, digging in her handbag for her Brownie box camera. "Let Aunty take a picture first."

"Oh, Aunty, not now," said Buzzy.

"Now look this way and smile, everybody," she said. "Tookie, don't slouch. Bobby, move a little bit so Aunty can get all of the chicken. That's good. Mahi, don't play with your chopsticks."

"Oh, for crying out loud," said Uncle Joey. "Just take the picture so we can eat."

"Just one picture," she said. "While the food still looks good."

He should have known it didn't do any good to complain. At every nine-course dinner, as far back as I can remember, Aunty Nona waited until the food came out and we were ready to dive in. Then she'd make us wait while she took a picture. In all her photos, our heads are chopped off, but the food looks great.

One small click at last, then another just to be sure, and then we grabbed our chopsticks and the real clicking began.

"I can help myself," I said to Aunty Nona, who was piling chicken on my plate.

"Here's another good piece," she said, sticking her elbow in my face. She transferred a piece of chicken from her plate to mine as if doing me a favor. According to tribal law, I now owed her the duty of eating it.

"No, no, Aunty," I protested. "Please. I have enough. I won't be able to eat what's coming."

"Don't worry," she said. "Take your time. You have all night. Besides, you're still young and skinny. You don't have to watch your weight like me." She laughed. Only when she was trying to feed me did I suddenly become too skinny. I leaned against her elbow, but she leaned back harder and the chicken thigh fell on my plate.

I hoped my favorite dish, the oyster rolls, would come out before I was stuffed. When Aunty Nona wasn't looking, I slipped the chicken thigh onto Uncle Joey's plate. I knew if I ate slowly, the food on our table would be gone before Aunty Nona could feed me more.

I looked around the room. Everyone seemed to be talking and eating at the same time. The voices, chopsticks, and bowls sounded like sand and gravel in a cement mixer.

Soon the chicken was gone. Frankel proclaimed the empty platter was to be used for the bones. We passed the plate around. Uncle Joey put the dish of bones down in front of me.

"Why did you put it by me?"

"I thought you were on a diet," he said. "Just shut up and eat."

"We forgot to toast the chicken," Tookie cried. Uncle Joey poured Scotch from the bottle on the table. I stuck out my empty jigger, which Aunty Nona filled with tea.

"To the chicken."

"To the chicken."

"To the chicken bones."

Now the hot dishes were coming out fast, along with

small hills of steamed rice. Roast duck with crispy red skin. Shrimp and crab on mounds of vegetables. Shiny black mushrooms, elephant ear fungus, bamboo shoots, and thick slices of abalone. Beetle's parents were going whole hog. I knew the food wouldn't run out. In fact, we would not be able to eat it all. If we did, Uncle Danny and Aunty Ah Oi would be disgraced because they hadn't ordered enough food. Sometimes I think the real purpose of the nine-course dinner is to show everyone that there will always be enough, that we will always have more than we really need. Uncle Joey, Aunty Nona, my father Kuhio—my whole family— would never tolerate a life of restraint, of just getting by.

The oyster rolls came out at last. I forked up two, even though I only had room for one. Aunty Nona put another roll on my plate. The oyster rolls were crispy on the outside, but when I bit into one, the juice oozed out and dribbled down my chin.

I watched Bobby eat. He caught my eye but didn't say anything, just winked. Tookie glared at me. I looked at my plate. I was beginning to feel like maybe I still had a chance.

I once wrote Bobby a letter that said, "Dear Bobby, I saw you making shi-shi in the empty lot. But I still love you. Get chance?" Before I could give him the letter, my mother found it and asked me what we'd been doing. I didn't see Bobby much after that, and then he was off to Oregon.

The waiter took away the plate of bones. I looked up and saw my father with his arm around Uncle Wing. My father's cheeks were red and his necktie was crooked. My mother sat talking to Aunty Lucy, but I knew she was keeping an eye on him. He and my uncle staggered across the room to toast the married couple. Two other uncles joined them in front of the head table.

"Goon bui! Goon bui! Pak til dow lau!" they shouted, and swigged and swayed.

———

After the oyster rolls came intermission. That was our chance to walk around and make room for more food. The emcee, Uncle Danny's best friend in the army, introduced the relatives and guests who had come from the mainland. Bobby, of course, the basketball star. Aunty Lucy, but Uncle Chin stayed in Sacramento because he hates to fly. A cousin and his wife from L.A. on their honeymoon. Nobody could figure out why they came *here* when they lived next door to Disneyland, where Beetle and Teena were going for *their* honeymoon. An aunty and uncle from Michigan. Their daughter, Cassandra, whom nobody recognized at first.

"Cleopatra's certainly filled out," whispered Aunty Nona.

"Her name is Cassandra," I said.

"Must be the air from the Great Lakes," said my aunty. "The cold air makes the fat form on your chi-chis." She stuffed a large black mushroom into her mouth, whole.

Even Bobby turned around to stare. I contemplated the last oyster roll, lonely on the serving dish.

———

Shark-fin soup followed the intermission. Frankel served the soup, since he was the oldest male cousin. By right, Uncle Joey should have served, but he declined.

"I need time to eat," he said, refusing to take the

ladle. Wei Ling held Frankel's necktie back so it didn't fall in the soup.

"Pass me your bowl," Frankel said to me. "Kiddies first." I wanted to wrap the tie around his neck.

After the soup came bowls of white steamed buns and thick, fatty slices of stewed red pork.

"This dish means long life," said Aunty Nona.

"No, it's red, red for good luck," said Frankel.

"Maybe Beetle and Teena will find gold in Disneyland," said Uncle Joey.

Long life, luck, money, a house full of children—no one at our table could agree. Everybody had an answer, but I knew if I pointed at the Chinese characters on top of a birthday cake, or at the sign over the entranceway to the restaurant, I would get the same responses. We were Chinese, but Hawaiian—and now Americans, able to vote—and many of us could not read or speak Chinese of any dialect. For all we knew, the Chinese words on the cake and over the door said, "May your teeth rot from all this sugar," or, "You are crazy to eat here." My family ignored such possibilities, content with thinking they were blessed with luck and every other bit of good fortune they could imagine.

I searched for a small piece of pork. I bit off the fat and spit it on my plate. Aunty Nona jabbed me with her elbow.

"That's the best part," she said.

"You can have it," I replied.

"Let's see if I can find you a better piece," she said, poking around the bowl.

———

I don't remember what course came next. I had lost count. All I knew was that I'd eaten too much and still had a long way to go. Even with Uncle Joey and Aunty Nona helping us out, we lagged behind the tables of big-eating adults. One of the uncles came over to our table and took away a platter to help us out. The bottle of Scotch was nearly empty, but we were behind in that too. The uncles at the next table were on their third or fourth bottle. We tried to catch up by toasting the rice, the waiters, the shoyu, the mustard.

Finally, we were done. Frankel let out his belt buckle two notches. Bobby loosened his necktie. His hair fell across his eyes like it did when we were kids playing in the empty lot next to the sugar-cane fields. I stared at his hands. I thought about how we played the piano together in the red dirt, his fingers running over mine. About my sweaty palms searching for the beat on his bony chest. About the cotton sunsuits I wore, the spaghetti straps that sometimes came undone. Once, I caught him staring, and when I looked down and saw my bare chi-chis, I grabbed the front of my dress and ran home. I knew I should tell him I had changed my mind about getting married, so he wouldn't fall in love with Tookie or a haole girl from Oregon. He'd only have to wait a few years. I'd tell him later, when the lights were turned down and the music started and he asked me to dance.

"Look, Mahi, you spilled gravy all over your nice dress," Aunty Nona said to me. "I told you to open your napkin up all the way."

I rubbed at the spot with a napkin dipped in water, trying not to make it look like I had gone to the bathroom down there. Another platter full of bones sat in front of me. Buzzy stirred the bones and fat and gravy into slop.

"Stop that. Stop that right now," said Aunty Nona. "Take away the bones," she said to the waiter. "And bring us some boxes for the leftovers." She bustled over to the younger children's table to gather up their half-eaten platters of food.

I scrubbed furiously and blew on the spot, trying to evaporate the stain now spreading wider and wider across the front of my dress. The band was tuning up, but my father was already dancing with a red-faced Beetle. Nine courses plus two bowls of saimin weren't enough to keep my father down. My mother had folded up all the dirty napkins at her table, and Aunty Lucy was doing most of the talking now. Tookie, Rhoda, the slut, was stroking Bobby's sleeve and whispering something to him. Her lips touched his ear now and then. Uncle Joey leaned back in his chair and belched. Beetle finally broke free of my father and ran to give his new wife, Teena Lum-Tong Wong, a long, hard kiss, as if he were afraid she would disappear.

Putting in the Pig

Don't ask me about putting in the pig, just hope it doesn't rain. Tell Buzzy to get up so he can mow the lawn. I know, he did it once before, but he needs to do it again. Tell him not to bang the mangoes this time, and don't run over the soyu beans I worked so hard to plant. The back yard was so full of rocks, Kuhio had to buy me topsoil, and look, now the imu takes up half the space. If you want to help, clean up your room or go outside and watch. But stay away from the imu; the fire is real hot. Who ate up all the rice last night? I promised Buzzy fried rice for breakfast. Now how am I going to make it?

Don't ask me about the pig anymore. You can watch them put in the pig as long you stay out of the way. Pigs are no fun anyway, they just run around in mud and eat slop and then you have to catch them and take them to the slaughterhouse. What fun is that? Not me, I'd rather buy the pig already clean, but not your daddy, he has to pick out the pig himself, make sure he's got the right one, nice and big and not too fat.

No, I don't know how many people are coming. We invited three hundred, but they don't know how to R.S.V.P. They think R.S.V.P. means show up if you want and bring everybody. But that's okay; that's why we're having a luau instead of a Chinese nine-course dinner. You had a baby luau too. And so did Buzzy and Benjie. Of course you don't remember yours, you were only one year old, but you remember Benjie's. Yes, you do. That's the one where you painted my lipstick all around your brother's eyes and I gave you good lickings. Now you remember.

Oh, I hope we have lots of leftovers so I don't have to cook for a while. At your luau, we had hardly any food left, so many people came. This time for Nani, I told Kuhio, make sure we have enough.

After breakfast you can help me clean the toilets. They smell so hauna, with people over here every night to help. We have to clean the toilets now, and then one more time tonight.

I wonder if we have enough opihi. So hard to get opihi now because of all the people washing off the rocks when they go to pick the shells. But you cannot have a luau without opihi, doesn't look good. Lucky thing Aunty Hannah Mele got some for us from her Maui cousin, nice big ones. Nona can serve them, so nobody takes too much. That way we'll have enough to go around, as long as she doesn't eat them all herself.

Oh, I hope it doesn't rain. At Tookie's luau it rained and rained and everybody got wet standing in line for the food, and they paid the band for the whole night but everybody went home right after they ate. Ho, so many leftovers that time.

What, the pig, still the pig? Sister, you have a one-track mind. I know who you take after. When Nona comes, you can go with her to get the flowers. They have to cut them at the last minute so they don't dry up. No, I said you can't help get the pig. Daddy and Uncle them left already for the slaughterhouse, didn't you see them go? Why don't you play with Nani, make sure she doesn't bang her head, and don't eat the haupia, that's for tonight. Okay, just one little bite.

I know, the toilets are stink, just hold your breath. Yes, you can watch the pig when it comes. We'll all go outside and watch. I hope Nona doesn't forget the butcher paper. You can help her decorate the table. We'll have ferns, orchids, plumeria, what did I forget? The pineapple, but not until later on, after the pig goes in. We still have plenty of time, the pig has to cook for eight hours.

I don't know why we invited so many people, it's not like Nani is getting married, but I couldn't scratch anybody off the list. It just better not rain; how are we going to fit everybody inside the garage? I hate to eat in shifts, that's cheap and no fun. It's better to invite only half as much, and then they can relax and stay all they want. But that's okay, we have a tent, good thing, and I told Kuhio, This time put it up *before* it rains, not after. We should have had the luau at Joey's house; he's all set up, has the hole dug, ready to go, but Nani's *our* baby. I just hope they don't step all over my green onions when they put the pig in.

Now, what did I forget? The chicken long rice, we put that together at the last minute; the poi, already mixed. The lomi lomi salmon, the squid. Oh, remind me to cook the rice. Big pot this time. I always forget the rice. What? Okay, you can throw banana leaves on top of the pig at the end, but that's all. No, the sweet potatoes are too heavy. You can't throw them in the imu like the leaves; they have to go in the wire basket all at once. But you can help load the basket now, just put the potatoes in one by one. Then I want you to help Aunty Nona. Just practice, then you know how, and when the time comes for you to give a baby luau, you know how it's done.

Look, here comes Nona, and just in time for breakfast. Bring out the Portuguese sausage and the eggs; no rice, but that's tough. Oh good, she brought some hot malasadas. What a big box. That's my sister. I can taste them already. How am I going to save my appetite for tonight? Go now. Help her carry her bag, so she doesn't drop the box. Then we better start thinking about lunch. They're going to be hungry after they put in the pig.

Chicken Fat

Nona claims it is the chicken tail she is eating, but the family disagrees. How can it be the tail? The tail is feathers, and the feathers are gone, plucked and thrown in the garbage. What she's eating is the okole, the ass, the part that sits on the ground. The tail, she says. It's the tail, not the okole. It's all the same, they argue. It's the tail, she says. And it's mine.

Nona stands in the kitchen over the pan which holds the chicken still hot from the oven. She holds the chicken tail between her fingers. It's from a small chicken, so one bite is enough. She eats it fast. Eats it fast because Anna needs to chop the rest of the chicken up. Gangway, everybody, here come the noodles. Mahi, get the salad out of the icebox. Buzzy, bring the paddle for the rice. Benjie, go wash your hands. Hurry up, Nona, you're not the only one who wants to eat.

When it comes to chicken or turkey, Nona is first with the knife. At Thanksgiving she eats the tail while her sisters fight over the neck. Who needs the neck? The tail is hers.

The turkey tail is bigger, fatter, and takes at least three bites. The kids crowd around and scream, Look at Aunty eating the turkey okole! The tail, she tells them. It's just the tail. How can you eat the okole? they ask her. How can you eat so much fat? You eat fat too, says Nona. You eat cow fat, pig fat. Everybody eats fat. I'm not the only one.

But she is. Nobody else in the family can stand the okole. Nobody else wants what's been sitting around who knows where. When Nona's not there, the okole stays on the chicken and gets cold. They eat the rest of the chicken and leave the okole sitting in the grease. Nobody wants it, not even if it's just the tail. That's Nona's piece, they say. Just leave it.

There's no good reason why they save the okole for her. Even when they pack it up for Nona along with the other leftovers, she never eats the chicken tail cold. She likes to feel the fat soft and hot in her mouth. What's the point in eating the tail if you can't eat it hot? That's why she can't wait until the table's set and everybody's ready to eat. She has to eat it hot, right out of the oven or off the barbecue. Or forget it, just forget it. Throw it out. Later on is just too late.

When the chicken comes out of the oven, Nona grabs the tail fast. She can never tell if one of the kids is going to grab it first. Oh, Aunty, they're always saying, clutching their stomachs, howling, acting like she's eating slop. Oh, Aunty, you make it look so ono. She never tells them they're right. She doesn't want them to think it's ono. She wants them to think it's junk. That way they'll stay away from the tail and she won't have to fight for what she wants.

When she was a kid, she had to fight. Her brothers and sisters always beat her to everything she wanted. She never had anything that was hers first and hers alone. She wore her sisters' clothes, played with their dolls, and read their books, and all the food was messed up on the serving dish before she got her scoop. The tail was the only thing that was hers. Right from the beginning they let her have it. They thought she was cute walking around the kitchen in her diapers with the chicken okole hanging out of her mouth.

Now her brothers and sisters act like they couldn't care less, but she knows they watch her eat. She knows they listen to her chew. She knows that when the fat finally goes down, it falls into many hungry stomachs. She knows they are watching and waiting for her to finish so they can start eating. She knows they'll wait, because they always have.

Let them wait. Let them give her a bad time. She grabs the tail before anyone can get to it. She gobbles it up in one bite. She feels the chicken fat explode in her mouth. She holds the fat in her mouth as long as she can and then swallows it before it gets cold.

Hapa Haole Girl

Annabel is hapa haole—half Chinese, half Irish. It's the Irish, the haole blood, that makes her hapa. Her hair is thick and long, the color of koa wood, dark brown with streaks of red. Her eyelashes curl like waves, and her eyelids fold back into tiny Venetian blinds even without the help of Scotch tape. Her skin looks like a vanilla ice cream cone licked smooth. When she dances Tahitian at school, her skirt rides on her hips like a boat in a storm. I watch the boys as they watch her with their eyes like balloons and their mouths wide open catching flies.

"Oh, Annabel, you dance so good," the girls say when she's finished dancing and the boys are still hanging around. But later the girls crouch to see if anybody's listening from the toilet stalls, and then the talk turns stink.

"Did you see her mother? The one with the red hair and the tight skirt."

"That's her mother? Wow, she sure has a fat okole."

"How you think Annabel got the hips to hold up her hula skirt? Not from her father."

"Lucky thing she looks like her mother. You should see her sisters. Real pake, just like their father. No hips, no chi-chis, no eyes."

––––––

But Annabel isn't that lucky. She got her mother's looks, but that's all she's going to get. Her mother is her father's mistress, not his wife. Annabel has three half sisters, who look like their parents, both Chinese. Annabel's mother will never be a Pang. She won't get to live in the house at Diamond Head, and she won't inherit the family restaurant in Kaimuki.. All she has is Annabel, who I am so jealous of I could scream.

"Am I a love child?" I ask my mother. If I can't be illegitimate, I want to be a love child.

She drops the chicken she's cutting. "Who told you that?"

"Nobody. Did you and Daddy have to get married?"

"Of course not," she says.

"Did you ever have a haole boyfriend?"

"What? Mahealani, who told you that?"

"Never mind. I have to go wash my hands."

––––––

What's she going to say when I tell her about Tommy?

––––––

Tommy is pure haole, the American kind, all mixed up. His father is a naval officer at Pearl Harbor. Tommy's hair is so blond it's almost white in the sun. He stands straight and tall, with his chin tucked in. The fur on his arms tickles when he comes near me. He likes to stand real close to people. One time he stood so close to the teacher, he stepped on her toes. She said, "Thomas McMurray, get off my toes!" "Yes, ma'am," he said, and saluted. The kids all laughed, and Tommy turned red like only a haole can get. I don't mind when he stands next to me, because he's tall, not like the local boys, who come up to my ears.

I try to picture what our children would look like. Would they have kinky brown hair and smooth pale arms, or straight blond hair and furry brown skin? I can't really see them in my mind, but I know hapa haole kids come out looking real cute. Maybe they will look like Annabel.

Tommy asks me to go to a dance at the base. Mostly haoles, service kids, will be there, but some of my friends have been invited too. My best friend, Ruthie Ito, for one. She's going with Stew Williams. Tommy catches me by surprise, and I feel guilty, as if he knows about my daydreams. He comes up to me after school and stares at me for a long minute before he speaks. His eyes are like blue marbles I want to win.

"I have to ask my mother." That's all I can say. I want him to smile so I can think of more, but he just nods, clicks his heels like a soldier, and walks away.

"Are you going?" Ruthie asks me.

"Maybe," I say. "I'm so sick of dancing with shrimps."

———

"Don't blame me," my mother says. "You know your father won't let you go out with a service kid."

"But his father is an officer," I say. "He's almost a general." I want her to say it's because Tommy is haole, so I can fight back. I want her to see how prejudiced they are.

Prejudiced. Ignorant. Old-fashioned. But she doesn't argue. She tells me to put the rice on the table and call in the kids.

I run to my room and slam the door, but after I cry, I don't feel so bad. I think about being close to Tommy. I think about the way he smells like warm bread and the way his hair tickles my skin. But I don't want to go out with him that bad. He's just part of a recipe I'm cooking. I want to be hapa haole, like Annabel. I want her hips, her hair, her eyes. I want to be Annabel, but not her mother.

Crackseed Sisters

You are home. I am so glad. Next time don't stay away so long. I have your favorite kind of crackseed, so we can sit and eat them while we talk. You might as well eat the seeds now. Don't wait until you go back to Oregon. You can take some crackseed with you, but it won't taste as good.

When I visited Lucy in San Francisco last Christmas, she brought down her tin can with the sleigh and the horses and the people wearing scarves, and she said, Oh, Anna, I've been waiting for you to come help me eat. When she ate crackseed in Nona's shop, they were so ono, she loved them, so I bought her five pounds to take back. But she said they didn't taste the same on the mainland. Not as sweet as before. Not salty enough, not as soft. But when we ate her seeds together, they tasted just right, even in California. We drank almost half a bottle of Blue Hawaii mix too. That stuff is so awful. I said, Why do you drink this? She said it reminded her of home, but she can only drink it when somebody comes from the islands to visit. Otherwise she gets homesick. We drank and talked story and ate up all her seed, so I had to send her more, and the next day I had a terrible stomachache. Ho boy, did she laugh at me.

Nona is always giving me crackseed. She knows which kind I like. She knows which kind you like too. When she heard you were coming home, she said, Here, take Mahi some sweet-and-sour cherry seed and li hing mui. I am always giving Nona mangoes and she is always giving me seeds. Enough, I told her. Give it to Lucy, give it to somebody else, not me. But she doesn't listen. She says, Save it for Mahi, when she comes home. You see how she's always thinking of you.

Crackseed sisters, that's what we are. Lucy, you, Nona, me. Aunty, daughter, mother, niece. We are sisters all the same. Talking story, eating crackseed, crying over all the sad and silly things we do. Our tongues grow raw from sucking seeds. We laugh until we cannot feel the pain.

Funny Kind

My mother said later it was a good thing we had gone to the bar where Buzzy was working, rather than just any old bar, in case we had seen somebody we knew. Otherwise we might have had to sit with them, and who knows what Aunty Lucy might have said or done? My mother had only agreed to a drink because she didn't want to upset Aunty Lucy, what with the divorce and all.

"We have to celebrate my freedom," Aunty Lucy had said to my mother. "And Mahi's twentieth birthday." She smiled at me. "But not here. Not iced tea." All around us women shoppers prowled through stacks of panties and bras, slips and nightgowns, at the McInerny's sale at Ala Moana. "Let's go where we can have a drink," said Aunty Lucy. "Let's go visit Buzzy in Waikiki."

———

We walked very slowly from the parking lot to the Mokulani Hotel, because my aunty was wobbling on a pair of new spike-heeled sandals. My mother and I worried for her feet, but Aunty Lucy wouldn't admit they hurt. Instead, she said, "I bet Buzzy can use the business this time of the day. They like to have women in the bar, you know. Brings in the tips."

"How do you know?" scolded my mother. She was being a bit of a prude, I thought.

"Oh, Anna, I know," said Aunty Lucy, talking a little too loud for the cool, hushed hotel lobby. She looked at me. "You have to be up on these things."

As we emerged onto the lanai, I decided my brother didn't have such a bad life, slaving away among the cattleya and Dendrobium orchids, Heliconia and hibiscus—flowers, ferns, and palms everywhere. Buzzy worked the day shift at the poolside bar. He swam and ran on the beach in the morning, took classes at the U.H. at night, lived on his tips, and saved the rest.

The bar stood under a thatched awning next to a pool shaped like a giant blue ear. Men and women in colorful bikinis lounged on white reclining chairs. Beyond the pool lay the sand, the beach Buzzy and I had played on as children, and, beyond that, the Pacific. In two weeks I would be a fifth of a century, and finally old enough to drink in a bar in Hawaii.

When my aunty saw Buzzy, she shouted, "Yoo hoo, Buzzy. Look who's here." As she smiled and waved, her black penciled eyebrows flew like crows over the freshly plucked fields where her old eyebrows had been.

All heads turned. Buzzy grinned and pointed to three empty stools. Aunty Lucy made me sit between her and my mother. Buzzy sauntered over.

"Hi, Aunty. Hi, Ma." A glance my way. "Sis." Then, in his best haole voice, he added, "And what may I get for you ladies?" I cracked up. My brother in a pink hibiscus shirt, hair slicked back.

"Shhh, be quiet. Everybody's looking," said my mother.

"I'll have a mai tai," said Aunty Lucy. "I heard you can get high real fast on those. And why don't you make Mahi a nice margarita. The slushy kind."

Buzzy shook his head and leaned with both hands on the counter. "You like me lose my job or what? Inspector could come anytime."

"But I'll be in Europe on her birthday," said Aunty Lucy. "I want to celebrate now. I have a lot to celebrate."

"Just use the bottle mix," my mother whispered to Buzzy. "No alcohol."

"And put plenty of salt on the rim," added Aunty Lucy. She pressed her long red fingernails into his forearm as she spoke. One of the nails popped off her baby finger, but she didn't seem to notice.

"Ouch," said Buzzy, rubbing his arm. "And what can I get for you, Ma?"

"A Coke. Somebody has to drive."

As my mother read the bar menu, Aunty Lucy elbowed me and opened her purse, a large plastic bag with purple and yellow daisies all over. She pointed at the miniature bottles of liquor she had collected on the plane ride from San Francisco. She had told us about the bottles earlier. Chin had taken all the booze when they divided up the house in Sacramento, so she was stocking up. Uncle Wing had fixed her up with a travel agent, who upgraded her into first class, where she could have all the liquor she wanted. Free, and "so many cute bottles to choose from." She hid them so the stewardess would bring her more. She saved the utensils and plastic dishes too, so I could take them back to college. Save them for my apartment. "We single girls have to stick together," she had said. "I can get more on the plane to Europe."

Aunty Lucy put her finger over her lips and pulled a small bottle of tequila from her bag. She sandwiched the bottle between her legs and the fold of her skirt. Buzzy brought the drinks. Aunty Lucy leaned over me and whispered loudly, "Save your swizzle sticks. They have the good kind here. Sturdy ones, not cheap stuff. Isn't this a nice bar? The men look rich."

"They're all haoles," my mother said. "I thought you didn't like haoles."

"Not me. That was Chin. That blond one over there is not bad. Too old for me, though. And see, what did I tell you? No wahines."

"What about those?" My mother nodded in the direction of the two-piece bikinis.

"Not worth looking at," said Aunty Lucy. "Too skinny. Bet you they go for Buzzy, though. Doesn't he look handsome in his uniform? I wonder if they have the little bottles here too. All the ones I see are too big. Open them up and then you have to drink them all. Otherwise they go bad."

She reached under her armpits and pulled up her bra through the fabric of her dress. She wore a strapless orange sundress that she had found on the 25-percent-off rack, but we'd had trouble finding her a strapless bra that would stay up.

"That's okay," Aunty Lucy had said as she looked in the dressing-room mirror at the falling bra. "I can stuff it with Kleenex."

"You're so bony," my mother had said. "Don't you eat?"

As we walked out of the store and into the sunlight, I noticed how much more hunched over her back looked now that it was exposed. She looked so happy, so pleased with herself, that I felt guilty. "You look great," I said. My mother must have felt the same way, because she added, "It's not such a bad color after all. Out here in the sun."

I had never seen my aunty's shoulders until that afternoon. She always wore sleeves. Even when we went to the beach she wore a white T-shirt over her bathing suit. I had never noticed how blotchy her skin was.

"Liver spots," my mother explained that evening. "Poor Lucy. She got old before she got young."

My mother stirred her Coke with her straw. The ice clinked and clinked. Finally she said, "Are you really going to wear this dress to the party?" She nodded at my aunty's faint cleavage. Uncle You Jook and Aunty Aggie were celebrating their fiftieth wedding anniversary with a Chinese nine-course dinner at the Royal Hawaiian later that week.

"Let them talk," my aunty said. "See what I care. That marriage is a fraud anyway. You know how You Jook is always fooling around. I wonder how many of his old girlfriends will be there."

"Lucy!" my mother cried. "You Jook is seventy years old! Besides, he's only talk. All mouth." She eyed me as she spoke, as if I were the one she was trying to convince.

"He's all mouth and hands. You know how hum sup he is. Always trying to feel us up when we were kids. Used to make me feel so funny kind."

"Because you let him. I told you to run away. Ma told you the same thing too."

I dipped my finger in my glass and played with the salt around the rim, wanting to drink, but not wanting to raise the glass just then.

"He doesn't even sleep at home when he goes out drinking," said my aunty. "He says it's too far to drive all the way to the other side of the island in the dark. Stays in town with Wing. Sometimes. Wing doesn't care what he does. Wing is too busy cooking up schemes."

"Kaneohe *is* far. Nobody likes to go over the Pali in the dark. Besides, how do you know what goes on? You only come home every once in a while."

"I know. I know, because people talk. They tell me everything. I go to visit them, and they feel sorry for me because of Chin. Because he doesn't come home with me. They say to themselves, 'Lucy no talk. Lucy no tell nobody. Who she going tell?' But I fooled them." She laughed. Gold fillings flashed from the back of her mouth like spotlights in a dark theater.

———

Lucille Afong, née Choy, was the only one of the four Choy girls they didn't call hau po. She didn't flirt like her sisters, didn't care how she dressed. She looked like a house-wife long before she met Chin and became one. Skipped the orchid and high-heel years. Even when Popo died and the girls split up the clothes, Lucy took the dresses that were gray and dark blue, the ones Popo wore to cook and clean in. The other sisters got the red and gold silk cheongsams.

"We offered to share the nice dresses with Lucy, but she didn't want," my mother said later. "I told her we should throw out the old-lady clothes, but she couldn't see them going to waste. She sewed up the slits to hide her thighs. Even Popo knew how to show off her legs."

——

Aunty Lucy unscrewed the cap on the bottle of tequila and poured me a shot.

"Lucy! What are you doing?" my mother said, but it was too late.

"Just for the taste. She has to learn how." Aunty Lucy giggled like a schoolgirl. She hoisted her bra, then rapped the bar with her palm.

"Oh no," my mother groaned. She covered her face with one hand and looked down at her drink. The men at the bar stopped talking. My aunty stood up. She swayed for a moment on her new spike heels until I grabbed her arm to steady her. She raised her mai tai, and in a voice so loud the people sitting by the pool turned around, she said, "Okay, everybody, how about a toast for my niece Mahealani. Finally old enough to drink."

I smiled weakly, looked at my mother for help, but she was still hiding. A haole man wearing a shirt with hula girls dancing all over it raised his shot glass. "To my li'l Annie," he slurred, and then the other voices and glasses chimed in. "To Annie," they crooned.

"They're drinking to you instead of me," I said to my mother. She shook her head. I knew she wasn't happy with what was going on, but I decided that that was her problem. Aunty Lucy was finally doing what she wanted to do for a change, and why not? I was ready to leave the nest myself. I took a quick sip of my margarita. Winced at the sour, then felt it bite. This was all right. Salty yet sweet, this first drink in a bar.

Aunty Lucy raised her glass and leaned her orange bodice in the direction of the man in the hula-girl shirt. "Nice man," she said. He started to get up and walk over to us, but Buzzy moved in, flexed his surfer arms, and said, "Watch it, brah. That's my aunty. Don't get ideas."

Aunty Lucy drained her glass quickly and set it down. "Suck 'em up," she said to me. Then to Buzzy. "A little more rum next time. And bring me a different swizzle stick."

————

My mother said later that it must have been the heat. The heat and all the shopping we'd done, the walking around on hot sidewalks that afternoon that made Aunty Lucy drink although she didn't usually drink. She couldn't hold her liquor and the drinking made her talk, made her say things she didn't mean about Uncle You Jook and Aunty Aggie. Just the heat, and the divorce. All Lucy got was half the house and a little alimony. She didn't know what had happened to the property Chin bought with his winnings at Tahoe, even though some of the money that helped him gamble came from selling some of Popo's jewelry. It was supposed to be for the business, the teak furniture Chin was going to import. Lucy knew she wasn't supposed to sell the family jewelry, but she did.

They all thought Chin was rich when Lucy met him, but what a lie. When they met at Uncle Sukey's retirement party, Chin was forty-two; Lucy was already an old maid at twenty-seven. Chin was quiet, smiled, nodded, and everybody thought, What a nice guy, better grab him while she still can. Their wedding dinner was the last party in Hawaii that Chin went to. He took Lucy to California to live, and when she came back to the islands to visit, she came alone. Chin didn't even visit his own family on the Big Island.

The last time I had seen Aunty Lucy was in Sacramento, when I went to visit during spring vacation my freshman year. She wore a gray sack dress made out of fabric that reminded me of gravel. She'd bought the material at a remnant sale at Woolworth's on one of her trips home. She used the same pattern again and again. Short sleeves, boat neck cut higher around the throat, and the waist and hips three inches too wide so the fabric wouldn't cling. She wore her hair pulled back into a tight, net-covered doughnut and shuffled around the house with a cardigan sweater thrown over her hunched shoulders.

When she saw my short red skirt, she frowned and said, "How can you sit down on the bus? Don't your panties touch the seat?"

She cooked my favorite Chinese food—black mushrooms with abalone, oyster rolls, squid with sour cabbage— all the food I craved and could not get in Oregon. Uncle Chin gobbled his food down quickly and then retired to the living room. He didn't say much, just watched TV and stacked up poker chips. Tall piles of red, blue, and white chips teetered on the end tables and the coffee table and on flat surfaces all through the house. If Aunty Lucy knocked them over as she vacuumed and mopped, she scooped them up and dropped them into a large Tupperware bowl, which she placed on the dining-room table, next to Chin's beer glass. When he went into the living room, he took the bowl of chips with him. Aunty Lucy sat and watched me eat.

"Take your time," she said. "Eat slowly so you can digest."

In the morning she served me soft-boiled eggs and

toast sprinkled with white sugar and cinnamon, like Popo used to make. She poured me a glass of tomato juice. I stuck out my tongue when I first discovered the juice was warm, blood warm.

"Cold juice isn't good for you," she said. "Too much of a shock on your system. Your body cannot wake up that fast. Me, I drink everything lukewarm—not too hot, not too cold."

Aunty Lucy collected maps. She spread them out on the living-room floor and pointed out the sights I should see on my vacation. She wanted me to see San Francisco, where my mother had gone to business school in the forties. She told me where the bus stops were. She knew all the routes and connections. She told me where to catch the trolley.

"Here's Fisherman's Wharf. You can go there and eat abalone steak. Here's Chinatown. When you go there, buy some almond cookies for dessert. I know how you like them. And you have to get up at four if you want to ride in with Chin."

"Aren't you coming with me?" I asked.

"No." She shook her head. "I have to stay home and cook dinner. I have to clean the house."

Aunty Lucy didn't drive. She didn't leave the house the whole week I was there, except when Chin took us to the grocery store. She didn't take me shopping for clothes, even though I knew she liked to shop. When she came back to Hawaii, she and my mother and I always ate dim sum and then went shopping. Aunty Lucy didn't buy much, a bamboo vase or a teapot for the house, a plain aloha shirt for Chin, but she enjoyed helping my mother and me pick out clothes. When we told her to try on something for herself, she always balked.

"Waste time, buying clothes," she said, "when I can make it cheaper myself."

After Chin lost his business and was looking around for another job, my mother told Lucy, "Why don't you and Chin move back to the islands? Joey always has something cooking. He can help Chin find a job in insurance."

"Chin doesn't want to come home," my aunty said. "He wants to stay on the mainland. My place is with him."

———

Aunty Lucy chewed ice from her third drink, a Blue Hawaii this time. She frowned as she crunched, as if the ice hurt her teeth. She was slouching now, propping herself up on her elbows and forearms. I wondered if the cold drink was sending a pain up her nose like the margarita was doing to mine, but it seemed childish to ask. Buzzy and my mother warned Aunty Lucy about mixing her drinks, but she refused to listen.

"I don't care," said Aunty Lucy. "I'm never getting stuck on one flavor again. People think you only like vanilla, so that's what you get for the rest of your life. Not me, I'm going to try everything. I'm going to travel, and I'm going to go anywhere I want and eat everything I can, and I'm only going to come back when I feel like it. Do you know this is the first time"—she poked my arm twice for emphasis—"the first time I have nobody to cook for? You don't know what it's like to be free. Not until you've been locked up. That's how it was my whole life, even when I was young and living at home."

"You were not locked up," said my mother.

"Almost," said my aunty. "I was the one who had to help Popo, because you went away to school and then Kuhio came along. Can't tell Nona what to do. Nobody asked what did Lucy want. I didn't have time to go out, and just as well, because what would I talk about? Nobody thought I could talk. Lucy such a good girl. Lucy so quiet." Her face was so close to her drink that she just tilted the glass in the direction of her mouth. Some of the blue liquid spilled down her chin.

"Maybe we should go," said my mother. "We need to find you another bra or take back that dress."

"I told you before, I'm keeping this dress."

"Well then, don't you want to take it off and save it for the party? You don't want it to be all stink."

"The party, the party. You're giving me a headache." She rubbed her forehead. She looked very tired, and the black around her eyes was melting at the corners. "Listen, Anna, the only reason they're having that party is to make money. They want to get back all the money they've been dishing out for years. Obligation, that's all it is. When's the next time they can do this? Their funeral. That's right. Obligation. That's why I'm not moving back to the islands."

"What? I thought you were coming back after your trip."

"Nope. I'm going to take the money from the house and travel until it all runs out. Serves the bum right. So chang with his money. Now I'm going to spend it all." She banged the table with her glass on the word "all."

Several heads turned our way at the sound of the bang. The man in the hula-girl shirt raised his glass.

"Oh, Lucy, Lucy," said my mother. "I know how you feel. Go and have a good time, but you have to come back."

"You don't know how I feel."

"But you can't just leave everything."

"Why not? I did it before, when I married Chin. You thought I was following him to California, but I was the one who wanted to go. It was my idea, not his."

"I didn't know that."

"You didn't ask. Nobody asked."

"I thought . . ."

"You thought I was the good wife."

"No, but . . ."

"No, don't deny. And now you think I'm crazy for wanting to have a good time."

"No I don't!"

"I can tell by the way you look at me. You think I'm too old."

I didn't look at my mother right then, but I could feel her desperation. This conversation was not going right. In fact, she should not even be arguing. Not with her newly divorced sister, not here in a bar, in the middle of Waikiki, not with Lucy getting drunk and throwing herself at strange men. How could she, my mother, let things get so out of hand? I don't mean to sound accusatory. I knew she was thinking this herself. If we had been at home, she would have found a way to end this conversation long before now.

I remember her telling me before Aunty Lucy arrived that people suffering from divorce are fragile. You have to be careful not to crack the shell. You have to let them think everything's going to be all right, because this will happen eventually. It just takes time. It's like when you're sick, you don't want people telling you you're going to die. You want to think you will get better, even though it might not be true. I liked the way she put things, but that afternoon in the bar I was confused. My mother seemed to have forgotten her own advice. Aunty Lucy was trying to look on the bright side of life, while my mother was the one who kept falling in the hole.

———

Aunty Lucy looked in the direction of the man in the hula-girl shirt, but Buzzy was standing in the way. A man in a tank shirt and shorts sat down next to her. He had a crew cut, dark glasses, and an outrigger canoe tattooed on his left biceps. His skin was slightly wrinkled around the eyes but baked an even brown all over. A cigarette jutted out of the side of his mouth. Without waiting for an order, Buzzy brought him a Michelob draft. I figured he was one of the regulars. Aunty Lucy fumbled through her bag for something. I hoped it was more tequila for me.

"You know," she said, as she piled the contents of her bag on the counter, one item at a time, "a person can change, but only so much. He is always the part of him that is himself." She pulled out small packets of salt and pepper, paper coasters, perfume samples.

"What are you doing?" my mother asked, but Aunty Lucy ignored her.

"You Jook is no different. With people like him, you know how they are right from the start." She pulled out foil packets of macadamia nuts and several swizzle sticks.

"With other people it takes a while, and when you find out, you think they have changed. But they haven't. They are just being who they are deep down inside."

Aunty Lucy finally found what she was looking for. A crumpled pack of Benson and Hedges. She pulled out a cigarette and turned toward the man with the outrigger-canoe tattoo. He lit her cigarette with his lighter. She patted his hand as he raised the lighter, then blew smoke in his face and coughed. She hacked and wheezed, and the man looked away. After she turned back to us, he moved to a stool on the other side of the bar.

"When did *you* start smoking?" my mother asked. She pressed her Coke into my aunty's hand. "Drink some of this."

"See, what I told you," wheezed Aunty Lucy. "Nobody knows me. You know how people talk about being born again? That's me. That's how I feel. Like I just came out of the egg. Trouble with you, Anna, is you think you're going to have a fiftieth-anniversary party too."

She offered me a drag from her cigarette. I shook my head no, but I was tempted. Right then a cigarette sounded really good. Half of me was thinking I might as well go with the flow, that maybe I could learn something from this adult conversation to which I was suddenly privy. The other half of me was feeling horribly disloyal, because my mother was clearly in distress. She was sitting there, stunned, not saying anything in response to Aunty Lucy's last, biting comment. I felt a sad kind of admiration. Even though my aunty's body behaved as if it was not quite right, her mind seemed to be mostly there. A lot of what she said made sense, even if she was saying what my mother didn't want to hear.

I signaled Buzzy. When I looked up, the man in the hula-girl shirt was holding up a fifty-dollar bill and pointing our way. Buzzy shook his head no to the man, yes to me.

When Buzzy walked up, Aunty Lucy said, "Give me a Singapore Sling."

To my relief my mother snapped, "No, it's time to go. You've had enough to drink." And then to Buzzy, "Bring us the check."

I was surprised Aunty Lucy didn't argue. Her abandoned cigarette lay dying in a pool of ash.

"I don't even feel sorry for Aggie," she mumbled. "She could have said something right from the start. Remember that, Mahi. All my problems come from keeping my mouth shut. And look at me now. Can't stop talking." She laughed, then started coughing again. I heard the sound of phlegm deep in her throat. "Oh, where did that come from?" she said in between coughs. "Maybe I'm allergic to the alcohol."

My mother reached behind me and patted Aunty Lucy on the back. "It's drafty in here. I hope you're not coming down with a cold." She spoke quietly, softer than I had expected. There were a lot of other things, worse things, she could have said. She looked tired, and so was I, all of a sudden.

"Why don't you meet me in Paris?" said Aunty Lucy to my mother. "You always wanted to go there. The tour guide told me there are lots of men on this trip. Rich ones, widowers, bachelors. I told her, Just don't make me room with an old fut who won't let me smoke. Put me in with somebody young at heart."

"That's right," said my mother. "You need to be around young people."

"I know. I was retired before I was even married, and now I'm single. Doing everything backward." Aunty Lucy smiled. At least she could laugh at herself, I thought. I caught a glimpse of the shy Lucy she must have been at one time. Thought of the beau she'd waited for, the one who was going to take her away from everything, her family, the islands.

"You know, I always hated my name," said Aunty

Lucy. "When people meet me, they think I should be funny, like Lucille Ball. But I can't even tell a joke."

"Maybe you could change your name," I said, then looked quickly at my mother to see if I'd said something wrong.

"I know what you mean," said my mother. "I didn't like my name either."

"You didn't?" I said. I'd never heard this before. They ignored me.

Aunty Lucy said, "Anna is a nice name. A good, strong name."

"I know," said my mother. "That's the trouble."

Aunty Lucy laughed as if that was the funniest thing she'd heard all day. My mother and I joined in. We laughed and Aunty Lucy coughed. Buzzy brought the bill. He had rung us up for $1.75, the price of my mother's Coke. He looked at my mother meaningfully, meaning she was not to question the amount. She handed him a twenty-dollar bill and said, "Keep the change."

"Thanks, Ma," he said, and validated our parking ticket.

Aunty Lucy slipped the empty glasses from our last drinks into her bag. She had already collected one, somehow.

"You can have two," she whispered to me. "For your apartment someday. We'll have a matching pair. Like sisters."

We helped her off the barstool and onto her feet. I carried her bag. Aunty Lucy limped into the lobby, where she begged to sit down. Her feet were swollen. "From sitting a little too long," she said. My mother and I looked at each other.

"Why don't you wear my slippers?" I said, pointing to my feet. I knew my mother's sandals were too small.

"Okay," said Aunty Lucy. Her eyes glittered a little, and I couldn't tell if that indicated pain or mischief. "You need the practice, anyway."

I wobbled at first, although I struggled to act as if I were in full control. They laughed.

"Just give me some time," I said. "I've worn heels before."

But I'd almost forgotten how. I hadn't worn heels since my senior prom. They matched the strapless white satin gown that my mother's friend Kimiko had sewn for me. I loved that dress. Kimiko had fashioned a giant obi sash for the dress, yet even with that wide bow, I'd looked slim at the waist and bosomy on top, especially when you added the double red carnation lei Weyland Pang gave me that night. Later that evening Weyland asked me to go steady, but I turned him down. Told him we needed to date others so we could get the most out of college. I guess I wasn't as crazy about him as I thought. He was put out, but I was ecstatic because he had asked. He had asked! When I returned home, everyone was asleep, including my mother, who usually sat up waiting for me. I managed to unhook the Merry Widow bra by myself, even though I had to turn the back around to the front so I could see what I was doing. But I couldn't undo the clasp of my pearl necklace and had to go to bed wearing the pearls. I felt foolish the next morning, having to ask my mother to release me from what was starting to feel like a chain around my neck.

———

After we got home from Waikiki, Aunty Lucy went to lie down while my mother and I fixed supper. We prepared her favorite food—squash soup, tofu stuffed with pork hash, and something special, mango crisp for dessert. But she slept through dinner, slept all the way through to the next morning. We turned the TV down low so as not to disturb her. Not that anything would have awoken her. Even her own loud snores and sudden snorts didn't disturb her slumber. My mother and I sat in the living room and listened to her reassuring sounds long after everyone else had crawled into bed with pillows over their ears. As we talked softly about the day, my mother crocheted a love-knot shawl for Aunty Lucy out of creamy wool, which she thought would tone down my aunty's new dress. Still later, in the privacy of my room, I wrote a poem about my senior prom—my satin gown, the high heels, Weyland's asking me to go steady. Kind of a first-love-that-is-abandoned-for-greater-things poem. I left out the part about the Merry Widow and the pearls. I decided later that I would give the poem to my aunty before she embarked on her trip. Her long journey away from home.

Pouring Tea

Your cousin pours tea on her wedding night. When you get married, you will pour tea for the elders, like your cousin is doing tonight. It is the family custom, Chinese style. Watch your aunty. She will show you what is right.

See how your aunty carries the tray with a pot of hot tea and her best china cups. Your cousin follows behind in her red silk suit. How soft she holds herself. Her whole body is saying, Look, I am not a girl anymore, I am old enough to love and be a good wife. Look at how her in-laws smile. They are feeling happy, because their oldest son has made a good choice. They are believing your cousin will listen and obey. They are trusting she will honor them and care for them and carry out the family tradition.

Observe how carefully your aunty places a piece of tong ko—a candied lotus root or a piece of squash—into the bottom of each teacup. How your cousin pours the hot tea from her mother's pot. How she pours like the stream after a big rain, full, never hesitating, but not spilling over the sides. Smell the tea. It is jasmine, with a fragrance sweeter than all the perfumes in the living room. So strong is the smell you have to breathe small. A little is enough. You hear a room full of swishing. Your cousin's silk, the tea, small breathing everywhere, except for your cousin. Her breath stays deep inside her and comes forth only to fall into cups. The promise she pours is more dear than all the china in the world.

Her mother's china is like ours. We bought our dishes together, in Hong Kong. All of us sisters, and for each one a different design. Chrysanthemum, rooster, tiger, plum. We bought china and cedar chests and jade and gold bracelets, not just for ourselves, but to pass on to our daughters. Someday what is ours will be yours. Your cousin is never alone. Your aunty guides her to her husband's father. Watch the elbows and knees. See your aunty lean forward to nudge your cousin. She kneels before her father-in-law. "Papa, yim cha." Father, please drink tea, your cousin says. All day long she teaches sixth grade. She talks to children in a very loud voice. But tonight she speaks softly. She does not need to yell, because everyone is listening, watching, waiting. For her. She is the one. See your aunty lean again, and your cousin backs up, bows from the waist. Do not worry. When it is your turn, we will teach you how. You will not be alone.

See how your aunty guides your cousin from father to mother, from uncle to aunty. Your cousin, who likes loud music and chews gum like a cow, does she not look truly beautiful for the first time in her life? Listen to her as she takes the pot and pours again. "Papa, tiam cha." Father of my husband, please have another cup of tea. In the old days she would be saying, For now I am your servant too. But we don't say that anymore. Today it is only custom. You do not have to believe, but what does it hurt you to show your respect? We will show you how it has always been done, how we poured tea for our mothers and fathers, because someday you may want to do the same. When you have a daughter of your own, you can show her what you know. What you know is what we know. What we pass on to you is more than custom, more than china and jade.

It is the way we married. The babies we had. The ones we lost. The work we did outside of home. The waiting. The cooking. The love we gave even without getting. The listening. Always the listening and forgiving. The teapot always hot and full.

After the elders drink their tea, they place red li see in their cups for good luck. Your cousin collects the cups one by one. She holds each cup with both hands and bows. "Do chiah. Do chiah." Thank you. Thank you. All the li see money is now hers to spend. She must use the money only to buy sweets.

Someday you will inherit your mother's china. Use her delicate teacups and all the dishes she bought, washed, saved all her life. You will hold her teacup in your hands. Feel the smooth lip of the china. Appreciate the way this fragile body has endured. Remember how we stood behind your cousin. How we will stand for you.

Spoon Meat

On the day we left the cottage in Waikiki and moved to a new subdivision in the sugar-cane fields above Pearl Harbor, my father, Kuhio, picked coconuts for the last time. Everyone came to see us off—Uncle Danny and Aunty Ah Oi, Uncle Joey and his girlfriend Tomiko, Aunty Lucy, Uncle Wing, Aunty Hannah Mele, Beetle, Frankel, Tookie. Even the aunties, uncles, and cousins from the windward side were there. Our DeSoto and the other cars were packed and ready to go. A caravan of uncles would follow to help us unload our furniture and clothes. Aunty Lucy brought cold beer and pupus for the workers. Uncle Joey brought a cage of homing pigeons, which he planned to let out at our new house to see if they could find their way back to Honolulu.

Aunty Nona gave us leis that she'd made the night before. White stephanotis leis for my mother and father. Pink plumeria and crackseed leis for me, Juicy Fruit gum and Life Saver candy leis for Buzzy and Benjie.

"Leis, Nona?" said my mother. "It's not like we're moving to the mainland."

"Oh, but Pearl City is so way out," said Aunty Nona.

I didn't want to move. I didn't want to be a country jack. Neither did Buzzy and Benjie. We liked Waikiki just fine. For the longest time I thought Kuhio Avenue and Kuhio Beach were named after our father, because that's where we belonged. The beach was our playground. Our babysitters were the retired haole couples with lobster-red skin who strolled on the sand and patted our heads, and the old men who played cards on the picnic tables under the spreading hau trees. Only a few hotels lined Kalakaua Avenue— the Royal Hawaiian, the Halekulani, the Moana. But other hotels and apartment houses were starting to appear between the beach and the Ala Wai canal, replacing small white cottages like ours.

"It's getting too crowded," my father had said. "Not like the old days." Besides, he had just started a new job welding sheet metal for the navy. If we lived in Pearl City, he wouldn't have to drive so far to work.

"You kids will have plenty of room to run around," he said.

Buzzy and I ran barefoot everywhere—on the hot sand, on our gravel driveway, on the asphalt and concrete. Monkey Toes, they called us. We took after our father, a good tree climber because of his long toes and tough luau feet. "The main thing," he said, "is to think with your feet, not just your hands." The neighborhood boys didn't believe us at first. How could a couple of pake kids like us have a father who climbed for coconuts like a real kanaka?

"Come on, kids," my father signaled to Buzzy and me. "Let's go pick coconut. One last time."

"Not now, Kuhio," said my mother. "Everybody's ready to go." But he ignored her. He kicked off his rubber slippers, stuck the handle of the machete into his mouth, and backed up the driveway to get a running start.

Three giant coconut palms shaded the front yard. They lay back like well-used lawn chairs, relaxed from having been mounted so many times. My father pointed at the most upright palm in the center. Buzzy and I nodded and crouched before the other two. I ran one foot up the trunk before I fell back. Buzzy scrambled two feet farther. My father swung his arms and legs up the tree like an orangutan and started hacking coconuts. The uncles and aunties cheered, and the cousins scattered like pins to gather the husky brown balls bouncing and rolling on the ground.

"Enough already!" my mother cried. "We're moving, not going to a luau." But she laughed as she said this and joined us in the roundup.

My father knocked off several green coconuts and climbed back down. He punched holes through the eyes, and we shared the sweet milk, tipping our heads back to get every drop. Then he cracked open the soft shells. The flesh inside was moist and tender enough to eat with spoons. We sat on the wall next to the hibiscus and bougainvillea hedges—kids, aunties, and all—and shared the spoon meat. My father saved four of the older coconuts to grate for haupia pudding. The uncles and neighbors gathered up the rest, and we piled into the DeSoto and led the parade to our new house in the fields where sugar cane once grew.

Looking for Bodies

I look for the dead bodies, the ones from the ships at the bottom of Pearl Harbor. The voice on the loudspeaker talks about the oil leaking from the ships. The oil means the ships really exist. But oil is not enough for me. I look for blood. I want to see the bodies.

I try to imagine being trapped in the U.S.S. *Arizona* at the bottom of Pearl Harbor. Makes me mad they didn't raise the ships. Just let them rot. Bodies, ships. I do not like to think about being underwater for twenty, thirty, a hundred years.

Our teachers take us to Pearl Harbor every year. I am tired of the same excursion. Our boat floats on dark water. The water is dark because of the leaking oil. The voice on the loudspeaker talks about how we got caught off guard on Sunday morning, December 7, 1941. About how the Japanese planes sneaked up on our ships. About how the ships went down so fast almost no one could get out. About the ships too heavy to lift, but they make good graves. About the dead bodies, trapped. I listen, but I don't believe. Every time we go to the harbor, I search the water for bodies.

After the boat ride, we get on the bus and go to Ala Moana Park for lunch. By the time we get back to school, I am hoarse from singing "Ninety-nine Bottles of Beer on the Wall." By then I have forgotten about the dead sailors at the bottom of the harbor. The same thing happens every year.

———

I live in Pearl City, and I go to school down by the harbor. My school stands next to an old Japanese graveyard. When we pass the graveyard on the way to school, my friends warn me to cross my fingers. They tell me to look for the smoke of the dead souls rising. They say I must not point at the graves. I must respect the dead. If I point, I have to bite my finger hard.

———

At school we have air-raid practice once a month. When the sirens blow, we are supposed to crawl under our desks and cover our heads. But our teacher, Mr. Chen, says, "Don't hide under your desks. Stand up and look out the window toward Pearl Harbor. This will be the last thing you'll ever see, so make it good."

Mr. Chen forces us to choose between democracy and Communism. "Would you rather be Red or dead?" he asks again and again. His question makes me mad. I know the "Star-Spangled Banner" and the Pledge of Allegiance to the flag. I was born in America. I am willing to fight. I know what I would choose.

"Are you sure?" he says. "If you fight, you die. This

island is a peanut in the middle of the ocean. Ask the people at the bottom of Pearl Harbor. What do you think they would have chosen?''

Mr. Chen makes me choose, but I'm not sure about my answer. And he won't tell me if I'm right.

———

I look for the bodies in the harbor every year. If I could just see them, maybe they would tell me something, I don't know what. But there are no bodies floating on the water. No bodies, no blood, just oil. One day they build a floating monument, but that isn't proof. The voice over the loudspeaker tells me the dead are buried forever in solid steel, but that isn't the answer I want.

———

On Saturday afternoon I walk past the graveyard on my way to the theater for the monster and samurai movies. Before the show starts, I buy a bag of kakimochi, some stink cuttlefish, and a Big Hunk bar to eat while watching *The Zombies of Mara Tau.* When the zombies kill men and women and carry them into the sea, my friends scream and I hold my breath. If I can hold my breath long enough, maybe the people will live. But I can never, never hold my breath so long.

I am exhausted after the monster movie and I want to go home. Ruthie Ito begs me to stay and watch the samurai. She promises to translate the Japanese, but mostly she screams. Not because she is afraid, but because she is in love, with Hashizo, the handsome samurai who leaps the highest and kills the most men. Hashizo finally loses a battle. He cannot live with his shame, so he commits hara-kiri. He stabs himself in the stomach with his sword, draws the sword from side to side, and his guts fall out. He grunts only once. His face does not show pain. My stomach aches. I close my eyes and clutch Ruthie's hand. I cannot hear what she says. I do not want to see the blood. I hear Ruthie crying. And then I am crying too. The movie ends.

After the show Ruthie and I link arms and pass the graveyard again with our fingers crossed. All the way home, we talk about the samurai. I ask her, How come they have to die every time? She doesn't answer. She talks instead about Hashizo's dark eyes, about the muscles in his arms, about his girlfriend, the one who cries over his dead body in the end. Did you see the way he kissed her, says Ruthie. Did you see him fight? Did you see his face when he committed hara-kiri? He's the best, she says. Nobody died as good as him.

Five Hundred Steps

When I saw the rising suns on the wings of the planes flying over our house, I knew it was the Japanese, and I knew where they were going. I ran up the hill, to the top of Pacific Heights. From there I could see Diamond Head, Waikiki, all the way to Pearl Harbor. I saw the planes. I heard the bombs. I knew then we would soon go to war.

I had just come home from delivering the Sunday *Advertiser*. Your popo, your mother, and my other brothers and sisters were still inside. The road to the top of the hill wound around and around, so I climbed the steps. Only the kids took those steps. They went straight up the side of the hill, through the woods. I counted them once. Supposed to be five hundred, but I counted only four hundred something. I forget exactly now. I wonder if those steps are still around. They were made of concrete, but most of them were broken, and the trees and bushes had grown up around. It was like climbing through a tunnel. Not the easy way, but I was sixteen. I could run up those steps three or four at a time.

Your mother hated the steps, because her hair always

got caught in the branches and she was scared of the dark. She used to say, "Danny, you go first," and when I ran ahead, she'd scream and cry.

"Take the road next time," I told her. But she wouldn't listen. She always had to go where I went.

———

Popo made me run after Danny. "Anna, go get your brother," she said. "Tell him to come home or your father will give him lickings." Goong Goong wasn't home. He slept at the shop on the weekends because the bank didn't open until Monday and he had to watch the money. So she sent me to get Danny because I was the oldest.

What about me, I wanted to say. Why should I run up the hill after him? But I couldn't talk back, not to my mother. So what if the Japanese planes attacked me while I saved my stupid brother. It was always Danny this, Danny that. Danny studying, Danny delivering papers, Danny getting ready for college. I cooked the rice, took out the slop. It didn't matter that Danny was younger than me, because he was a boy, the oldest son. That's how it was. Real Chinese style. Everything for the five boys.

I didn't see Danny go, but I knew where he went. Up to the top of Pacific Heights, to the little park, where you could see half the island. And I knew he ran up the steps because that's how we went up the hill in those days.

Oh, I didn't want to go up those steps by myself, but Popo wouldn't let the other kids go with me. One slip and I could fall and break my leg and they wouldn't be able to find me in the dark. I had to crawl on my hands most of the way, because the steps were so broken. I was afraid my hair would get caught in the bushes and I'd be stuck forever.

Danny loved to scare me. He used to oink like a wild pig and point out their footprints. I had to count the steps out loud to keep my mind off the pigs, but I always lost track after two hundred. Seems like there were a thousand steps, not five hundred.

I knew Danny would get to the top of the hill before I could stop him. He loved to watch the airplanes. We all did. Every time somebody left the islands, we drove to the airport to say goodbye. We watched all the planes take off, not just the one. Every time I smell the exhaust from airplane engines, I remember how the hot air blew through the old terminal, right up my muumuu. I wanted so much to ride the airplane, but Danny was the one who would be going to the mainland for school, not me.

The bomb exploded when I reached the opening in the wall that led to the steps. The explosion came from far away, up on the hill, and I knew I had to hurry. I crawled through the hole in the wall behind the second date tree. I wanted to turn back, but when I heard the bomb, I knew I had to find Danny and bring him home.

———

When I reached the top of Pacific Heights, the army trucks had already arrived. A soldier with a rifle shouted at me, "Hey, boy, did you see where the parachute landed?" I didn't see any parachutes, but I saw where the bomb had fallen—through the roof of a garage. The garage burned and smoked, and the people in the house came running out, trying to figure out what was going on. I decided to take cover behind the bushes.

That's when I spotted the unexploded shell lying on the ground. It was a nice big one—longer than a football, but narrow. I bent down to pick it up. I wanted to take it home for a souvenir. All of a sudden somebody yanked me by the collar. I looked behind. It was the old Japanese man who took care of the park. I'd seen him before, pruning the trees and picking up garbage. He was just a retired guy with nothing else to do. He said to me, "Son, leave that alone. Don't you see all those people running? You better get out of here." That's what he said. I remember every word.

I turned around and took off down the road. The steps were steep so the road was always faster going down. But I was so scared I ducked into the garages every time I heard a dog bark. It took me a long time to get home.

Popo stood in the driveway, with her chopping cleaver in one hand and a pot on her head. I started to laugh, but she shook the cleaver at me. "Where's your sister?" she said. "Anna ran up the hill to look for you."

————

I should have called Sueo to help me. Sueo Watanabe. He was my boyfriend at the time, and he was real strong, almost black belt. But there wasn't enough time. I had to go all by myself. I had to run up the hill fast, so I took the steps, because that's what Danny would have done. I figured if he could do it, so could I. I started out slowly, then I tried to run, but I kept falling down. It was so dark and the branches kept poking me in the face. So I got down on my hands and crawled. I didn't know I could crawl so fast. I couldn't see a thing, not the houses, not the road. You couldn't see anything from the steps, just shadows every-where. I couldn't see, but I could imagine. I thought I heard a mongoose, and wild pigs, bats, gorillas, tigers—everything Danny scared me with and more. I shouted, "Danny!

Danny, come back!'' all the way up the hill. I was so mad at him. I guess that's what kept me going.

When the second bomb exploded, I got up and ran. This bomb was much louder than the first. I was so scared, I ran right up those steps clear to the top. I didn't care if I fell. I didn't care about anything except finding my brother and bringing him home.

When I reached the clearing, I was so tired I fell down on the grass. But I didn't stay there long. The old man's pruning shears lay on the ground, right by my head. I wondered why he had left them there. And then I saw the body. Blood dripped down his face and chest, and his leg, his leg wasn't there. At first I thought it was Danny. Oh no, I thought, but his hair was white. I saw the body and the leg and then I saw the big hole in the ground and then a soldier came up to me and said, ''Where did you come from?'' He didn't know about the steps. You couldn't see them unless you knew where the opening was. And then another soldier ran up and said, ''Leave her alone. She's just a local girl.'' There was so much going on, they forgot about me.

I don't know why I didn't cry. I hate the sight of blood. But I had to find my brother; I guess that's why. Everybody was running around. I heard they were looking for the Japanese, for the parachutes. I ran around the park and along the street at the top, but I didn't see Danny anywhere. I thought maybe he went home, and then I remembered how we always ran down the road. Danny could run real fast. He could be home by now. But I didn't want to take the road down. I was afraid I would get bombed in the broad daylight. I mean, he didn't have a leg! I felt so sorry for the old man. I still remember all the blood.

So I took the steps back down. Not even Danny went

back that way. I'm the only one who did it. I was the first. Looking back, I don't know how. Maybe it's because I had so much on my mind. I told myself Danny could run faster than anybody. I kept saying out loud, "You can do it, you can do it," and I didn't know who I was talking to, Danny or me. I thought about the old man and the blood and his leg, and I got so mad at Danny for not thinking about the rest of us before he took off. I thought about the soldiers and the planes and the bombs. I thought about Sueo and how my parents didn't like him because he was Japanese. The steps were nothing compared to all that.

If only then we knew about Wing. How he wasn't really Chinese after all. Then they would have seen how stupid it was. Even Joey went out with Japanese girls. But he was younger and by the time he started dating things had changed.

Have you ever held a photograph up to the sun and looked at it from behind? That's how it was. Everything was backward and inside out. I knew Danny would go away to fight, not to study mechanical engineering. And Sueo and I would never get married, even if Goong Goong said yes. It wasn't up to us anymore.

———

I found your mother behind the second date tree, sitting in the hole in the wall, all scratched up and trying to catch her breath. When she saw me, she jumped all over me. She punched me and yelled, *"Where were you?"*

I said, "Take it easy, take it easy. You made everybody scared."

"They're scared about you," she said, "not me." And then she started crying and shaking all over. And then I knew she had run all the way up the steps and then all the way back down. I held her tight and we sat down on the curb and cried. When we got home, Goong Goong scolded us—he had closed the shop and come home—and Popo fed us jook while we listened to the radio. We listened day and night until finally, just like I knew, President Roosevelt declared war.

The schools closed down, so I volunteered to work for the U.S. Engineers. They sent me to Hanauma Bay to dig a trench, a big long trench in the sand. They didn't tell us why we were digging the trench, and I didn't ask. The soldiers walked up and down the beach with rifles while we dug. They kept looking at the sky and out to sea. One of my buddies said they were going to bury dead bodies in the trench, which made us all laugh, because it wasn't funny. I think they buried ammo there. Ammo and guns, in case the Japanese captured the island.

A few months after the attack on Pearl Harbor, I worked on the U.S.S. *Arizona*. The ship was so heavy, they couldn't raise it. The metal was real thick, but you should have seen it, twisted, terrible, like a tin can. I helped another guy pump out the gas that had built up inside the ship. I tried not to think about where the gas came from. We worked from a small boat. The water in the harbor was pretty rough that day, and I had to hold on to the sides so I wouldn't fall into the stink, oily water. The men in a nearby boat were scooping debris out of the water. I saw a foot with the boot still on. I didn't go back to Pearl Harbor after that. I have never visited the *Arizona* memorial.

———

Goong Goong sent me to San Francisco after I graduated from high school. He was afraid I'd elope with Sueo. I went to business school and lived with a Chinese couple. They were so chang. I paid them for room and board, but they never gave me enough to eat. I was so hungry I scraped the hard rice that burned and got stuck to the bottom of the pot. I mixed the rice with hot water and ate it over the sink before I washed the dishes. I missed my family, but I couldn't go back home until I finished school. In those days, you couldn't just fly back and forth.

I never saw Sueo again. He fought in the war, along with the other local Japanese boys. I heard he lost his arm, and then when he got out, he married a nurse, a girl from the Big Island. After that, I told my girl friends I didn't want to hear any more.

Danny got drafted. He came to visit me in San Francisco before he shipped out. I cried when I saw him in his army uniform. So handsome and he was my brother. "Let's go eat, Sis." That's the first thing he said. I took him to Chinatown because he was so ono for rice. All they fed him in the service was potatoes, potatoes. He said, "Eat up. Uncle Sam is paying for this." So we ordered five dishes for just the two of us, and three big bowls of rice, and we ate it all up, like there was no tomorrow.

Tough Tripe

Uncle Wing pokes his chopsticks into the bowl of boiled tripe. He chooses a thin slice that flaps between his chopsticks like a white flag.

I ever tell you about my German friend? My unit was assigned to escort German prisoners from the States to England after the war. I met Franz on the ship. He was from the German Army, not a Nazi. Smart guy. Used to be professor at Oxford. He taught me to speak a little German. Enough to help me get by when I was stationed in Munich.

Wing dips the piece of tripe in shoyu laced with hot red pepper juice. He waves his chopsticks around in the air while he talks.

One day I was standing in the train station at Frankfurt. I heard somebody call me. Ving! Ving! So funny. I looked around and there he was. My friend the professor. Just out of jail from Liverpool. Can you imagine, still in his prison clothes! We hugged and laughed. Then we talked. Him in broken English, and me with my lousy German. He took me home to meet his family. They fed me Wiener schnitzel and sauerbraten, and we drank lots of beer. They invited me for Christmas, so I went. They didn't care I was Hawaiian Chinese. They still send me a Christmas card every year.

Wing stuffs another piece of tripe in his mouth. This piece is thicker than the first and tough to chew, even though beneath its tight skin the tripe is full of holes.

They tried to shanghai me when I was a kid. Not the Germans, my own family. I heard my uncles talking. They were going to send me to China by boat. They wanted me to grow up to be real pake. Ask your father, Kuhio. He knows what I mean.

Wing chews slowly and swallows hard. He takes a long sip of beer.

I was only five, and I had short legs, but I ran as fast as I could. I hid in the hills, where they couldn't find me. From up there I could see the harbor and the Matson liner. I hid until the ship left the harbor, then I went back to the house. I thought my uncles would give me lickings, but they didn't. They were so happy to see me they cried. Everybody cried. Me too. They never tried to shanghai me after that.

He eats the tripe, one slice after another, thin and thick, talking until the whole bowl is gone.

Avocado Uncle

The trouble with Sukey was he couldn't say no. No matter what people asked for, even if they didn't ask, if they just acted like they were ono for something he didn't have, Sukey showed up at their house the next morning with what they craved—a giant Chinese squash for soup, a long and tender bittermelon, ready to cook with salted black beans and eat over steamed rice. When a customer told him the watercress he brought her had the biggest leaves and sweetest stalks she'd ever eaten, from then on Sukey gave her the best bunch of his lot and delivered it to her house first, before the sun heated up his truck. That's why people bought vegetables from him, not just because he drove up and down the streets of Kakaako every day like the ice cream man, but because they knew Sukey, the Chinaman, would always bring them the best. They paid him, of course, but he charged them only a few pennies for what would cost five or ten cents at a store in downtown Honolulu.

Even on the day after Sukey's sister Patty and her baby died, Sukey did not stay home and mourn with the family.

He had done his share of crying the night before. That morning he went out early, as usual, to peddle his vegetables. He knew his customers counted on him, especially the Japanese family who could not pay him every time. No matter. He always stopped at the Miyakes' house last and traded his leftover vegetables for ripe avocados from their trees out back. That way they didn't have to pay him. But that day, instead of avocados, the Japanese family gave Sukey their baby. It was a boy, but they already had four boys and three girls they could barely feed.

When he pulled up to their house, he heard the bulldozers and shovels in the empty lot next door. The Miyakes had planted their avocado trees on land they did not own. Now the trees lay tangled in heaps of dirt and rock with their roots choking in the air. FUTURE HOME OF AKAMAI CONSTRUCTION COMPANY, a sign on a stick warned passersby.

"You take baby," the mother shouted over the sound of gravel and whining truck gears. "You take. No can feed."

———

What could Sukey do? How could Sukey say no? He knew how poor the family was. That's what he told himself at the time. That's what he would tell his brothers and sisters later that day.

"I no like see the baby *make* die dead," he would say to them.

Talking about the dead would make them cry. Make them sad again for their youngest sister, Patty, who had passed away the day before. She had died giving birth, and she wasn't even married. Her baby had died too. A baby boy.

How could they argue with him when he brought the

Miyake baby home? They would see the baby was hungry. But just in case, he wouldn't tell them everything, such as which family gave him the baby and that the baby wasn't Chinese.

———

The Japanese woman's eyes stung Sukey like darts as she shoved her baby into his arms. The baby was only a few days old. Sukey held the baby like an overripe melon, careful not to squeeze too hard. He stuffed the bunch of watercress he had been holding into the woman's shaking hands. Now they both had something—baby, watercress—to hold.

"You make watercress soup," he said. "Tomorrow I bring you squash."

In some ways the hardest part was losing the avocados. The avocados Sukey got from the Japanese family were the best on the leeward side of the island. They were like baby footballs, bright green and smooth, no pockmarks on the skin. And they were sweet inside, so sweet everybody who ate them wanted more. Sukey's avocados were the best, and he never told anybody how he got them.

After work, Sukey often took avocados to his older brother's house. Avocados bulged from the pockets of his baggy shirt and pants. At thirty, Sukey was the youngest and shortest of the brothers, and he dressed as if he still expected to grow, several sizes too big and the sleeves and cuffs rolled up again and again. Plenty of good places to hide avocados.

As Sukey walked up his brother Khi Fong's driveway, the children shouted, "Avocado Uncle's here!" Sukey tossed three avocados in the air, one at a time, then threw one at the circle of neighbor children gathering around while he pulled another from his pocket. He juggled and lobbed the green fruit, one by one, until he had emptied his pockets and the avocados bounced in smaller hands.

"No can stay for dinner." He shook his head at his sister-in-law Puanani, who was pointing at the pot of soup on the stove. "Maybe tomorrow. Gotta go home. Gotta go water my avocado plants."

Sukey's avocado plants were his pets. He spent most of his free time taking care of them, at least until he brought the baby home.

———

Sukey lived with his older sister Wena and her six-year-old daughter, Kimmy, in the family house in Makiki. Their other brothers and sisters had moved out of the house one by one, leaving the place to Sukey and Wena. Kimmy's father, the bum, had run off, and Wena was lucky Sukey could help her out so she didn't have to work full-time, just in the cannery when the pineapple was ripe. Sukey did his best to act like a father to Kimmy, but there wasn't much he could do for Wena, who stayed up late, lying on the living-room couch in the dark, long after Kimmy and Sukey had gone to bed. Sukey knew what Wena would say when he brought the baby home.

"You can't raise him alone," she would say. "You can't have a baby without a wife."

"Oh, Wena, Wena," he would say, singsonging her name softly, like he always did, until she let him have his way. He'd called her Wena from way back. Wena was short for Rowena. When he was a baby, Sukey had shortened it to Wena. Sukey had named himself too. "He's sure cute," people said about him as he crawled around the family store. Sukey thought "sure cute" was his name. "Sukey when walk" were his first words, then "Sukey when eat." So Sukey they called him, instead of Wayne. All the other brothers and sisters, except for the oldest, Khi Fong, went by their American names.

Sukey grew up between the aisles of the family grocery store on Maunakea Street in Honolulu Chinatown. He grew up among the water chestnuts and lotus roots. He snacked on dried lemons and candied squash. The family let him run around loose while they waited on customers and hawked the specials of the day.

Nobody complained if Sukey threw the tangerines or rolled the passion fruit. Sukey made the customers laugh and feel at home. If Sukey the baby could squeeze the fruit, so could they, and they did and they liked and they bought. Later, when Sukey the boy showed his knack for selecting a papaya that would ripen sweet at breakfast time the next day, and then picked out three more papayas just right for the next three days after that, they said, "Hey, this kid can really pick." But Sukey the teenager had in mind something besides working in the family grocery store.

As soon as he could drive, Sukey loaded up the family truck with vegetables and headed for Kakaako. He drove up and down the back alleys and shouted out the windows of his truck, "Swamp cabbage! Watercress! Two cent only! Fresh pick this morning!" Soon the people had their money ready when he came by. His older brothers complained about how much business Sukey was taking away from the store. Sukey told his brothers the people he sold to didn't go downtown to shop, but his brothers wouldn't listen. They just liked to squawk.

———

On the day Sukey brought the Japanese baby home, his older brothers did not open up the shop. Instead, they went to Sukey and Wena's house. Just the brothers and the sisters, nobody else. All night long they had cried about their sister Patty and her baby, who had died earlier that day. Today they would meet again, to cry and also to talk. When Sukey got home they would decide what to do about the funeral for Patty and her baby. Under the circumstances, should they keep the funeral small, just for family? Or act like everything was normal and have a big one, followed by a Chinese dinner for everyone who came to the funeral? They knew Sukey didn't want to talk about Patty, didn't like to make up his mind about anything big, but this was a family matter. It had to be done, and Sukey had to be there.

When Patty had gotten pregnant, Sukey had tried to stay out of the family talk about his unwed sister. The family did not like the boy, a real good-for-nothing she met down by the wharf, no job, just hanging around, playing cards. When the boy found out Patty was hapai, he took off just like that. The family had argued about what to do, what to tell the neighbors, what to tell the cousins, the aunties, and the uncles. One sister without a husband—Wena—was enough. But two? They had finally made up a story about the husband, about how he was a rich, older man from China who had gone back to Hong Kong to sell everything, about how he and Patty had gotten married secretly, no fuss, no gifts, but then he'd died on the boat—food poisoning, of all things—and, talk about sad, the poor guy didn't even know he was going to be a father.

———

Sukey heard his family talking when he brought the baby home. He tiptoed into the kitchen, hoping to avoid them, but he knew he couldn't hide from Wena. She had lived with him long enough to recognize his sound—a bulldog when he was tired and hungry, a chicken when he was excited. The way he sounded today was different, more like a cat who has brought home a special snack.

Wena was already waiting for him in the kitchen. Pointing at the bundle Sukey set down on the table, she said, "What, more avocados?"

Sukey shook his head and unwrapped the cloth.

"Aiiyaa!" Wena screamed. "A baby! And it's still alive!"

"No yell," said Sukey. "You like wake the baby up?" But it was too late. Upon hearing Wena's screams, the rest of the family pounced from the living room, and the baby began to cry.

"See what I told you?" said Sukey. "You made him cry."

"Whose baby is that?" said Wena, looking very pale.

"I thought Patty's baby died yesterday!" said Khi Fong. He held up his cane, ready to strike.

"He did," said Wena, looking closer. "This is not Patty's baby."

"This is my baby," said Sukey.

"What do you mean?" said Wena, but Sukey refused to say more. He climbed on a stool and reached for one of Kimmy's old baby bottles at the back of the top kitchen shelf.

"Wash the bottle out good," said Wena. Sukey grunted and set a pot of water on to boil. While he heated some milk in another pan, the family grilled him.

"What are you doing going around stealing babies?" demanded Khi Fong.

"You better tell us where you got him from," said another brother.

"You cannot keep this baby, Sukey."

"Never mind," said Wena finally. "We can talk later on." She knew nobody could make Sukey talk when he didn't want to. She added, "Can't you see the baby's hungry? Hurry up with the milk. Here, give me the bottle."

The family crowded around as she held the baby in her arms and fed him.

"Look at him suck," said Wena.

"Eats like a good pake," said Khi Fong.

"But so skinny kind," said one of the sisters.

"Sure cute, though."

"Sure cute, like Sukey."

They pointed at the baby's eyes, scrunched into slits, like Sukey's when he laughed, and then at the baby's matchstick arms and legs, all folded up.

"A bird baby," said Wena, wrapping him back up. "A little chicken wing," she added, and they liked the name. Wing. Like Sukey, Wing was a good Chinese name. The family didn't know those were Japanese eyes that opened up slowly when the aunties cooed. And Japanese lips that sucked at the nipple Wena stuck in his mouth. Sukey might have told them the truth if they'd asked him then, right then, but instead Wena said, "Better heat up another bottle. This kid's a big eater."

Since the family had made up a husband for Patty, a rich one, even sending him away to die, lying about the baby was easy, although there were now two babies to account for. They would tell everybody Patty had died but her baby had survived. They would say Patty was so sad about her husband's death that she'd gotten sick and that's why the baby had come early, and that's why she had passed away, poor thing. And now Wing was all they had, and they would take good care of him. They would let Wing live with Sukey and Wena so Kimmy wouldn't have to grow up all by herself. Instead of a father and a mother, Wing would have six aunties and uncles. Six parents—ten, if you counted the husbands and the wives. Some kids were stuck with just two. That's what they'd tell Wing when he grew up. They would raise Wing as their nephew, their dead sister Patty's son, as real flesh and blood.

While they talked, Sukey shuffled about the house, preparing it for his baby. He lined the clothes basket with a rice bag and an old quilt for a crib. He swept the kitchen floor and scrubbed the bathroom sink and toilet. After the family left, excited about the new baby, after Wing fell asleep in his basket, after Wena and Kimmy went to the store to buy more evaporated milk, only then did Sukey finally sit down.

He selected an avocado from the ones he'd brought home the day before everything happened. Before Patty and her baby died. Before the avocado trees were cut down. Before the Japanese family gave him Wing. Such a long time ago, and yet this avocado was only now just right for eating. He sliced the ripe avocado in half and carefully removed the seed with his spoon and set it aside. He ate one half of the avocado slowly, letting the sweet flesh melt in his mouth. He ate straight from the shell—no shoyu, no sugar or pepper, nothing. In the morning maybe he would tell Wena the whole truth about Wing, but only Wena, he promised himself. Wena, that's all.

Sukey scooped chunks of the second half of the avocado into a small bowl, added some mayonnaise and pepper, and spread the mixture between two slices of whole-wheat bread. Usually he followed the avocado sandwich with a bowl of watercress soup or a pot of steamed squash. Wena had tried to cook dinner for him, but Sukey was very fussy and hard to cook for, because he wouldn't eat meat, so she finally gave up. When he opened the refrigerator, he averted his eyes so he wouldn't have to look at the raw meat Wena had put in there. A real pake was supposed to like meat, but Sukey didn't like food he couldn't hold safely in his palm while it was still alive.

But no more vegetables tonight. The avocado and the baby filled him up. He washed his bowl, then rinsed the avocado seed. He filled a small glass halfway with water, stuck three toothpicks into the middle of the seed, and placed it in the glass. He put the glass on the windowsill, next to the other jars of sprouting avocado seeds. He and Wena had argued about which way the seed should point. "The wide end should go down," she said, "so the seed will have plenty of roots." But Sukey wanted the seed to have room to breathe, so he put the wide end up.

Mana

When the trucks dumped gravel all over Lani Gerard's front lawn, I thought the neighbors were right after all. After his boyfriend Ambrose died, Lani must have gone crazy. He screwed sheet-metal plates over all the windows of his house. Small oval holes in the metal armor let in the air and sun, but I thought of him on hot nights when I clung to one edge of my bed so the other side could cool down. From my window I could see the lights from Lani's house shining like a thousand eyes. Not long after putting up the armor, Lani installed a fence. An expensive chain-link fence with barbed wire across the top and a remote-control lock on the driveway gate. He's crazy, the neighbors said. Loco, pupule, nuts.

We didn't see much of Lani even when Ambrose was alive. When we passed their house on the way to school, Buzzy ran ahead of me, shouting, "Better run fast. The mahus going catch you if you don't watch out."

I saw Ambrose tie paper bags around the mangoes on the tree in their front yard to keep off the bugs, and I watched Lani pick up the rotten mangoes that fell on the ground. But they never shared their mangoes with anyone. They stayed away from the block parties, and they didn't let us play in their yard. But Lani and Ambrose didn't bother anyone. Except for the loud music they played at night and the rusty scrap metal Ambrose brought home by the truck-load and piled in their back yard, having a couple of mahus on the block wasn't that bad.

"They go to work," said my father. "They pay taxes just like everybody. Leave them alone."

——

After Ambrose died and the fence went up, we never saw Lani come out of his house. We didn't hear music. The kids on the block ran back and forth in front of Lani's house, scraping their bats along the chain-link fence. Lani went to work early and came home late, in the dark, and he parked his car in the garage.

Buzzy was the only one who got close, because Lani hired him to mow the lawn. But Lani never paid Buzzy face to face. On the phone he told Buzzy where to find the money. Buzzy found dollar bills hanging from a thread tied to the papaya tree out back. Or taped to a cigar box buried in the back yard. Or stashed somewhere in the junk pile. The kids placed bets to see who could guess how Buzzy would get paid.

When the gravel trucks showed up, we called off the bets.

"No worry," said Buzzy. "I get plenty lawns to mow."

But that night I heard my parents talking after we kids had gone to bed.

"No look good, the way he's locked himself up," said my father.

"I hope he doesn't kill himself," said my mother. "How would we find out?"

I worried about what I'd heard for a week, until the afternoon Buzzy threw a gum wrapper over the fence into Lani's yard on our way home from school.

"What's the matter with you?" I screamed. "Do you want to make him mad?"

"Take it easy," said Buzzy. "What he going do?"

———

The next morning I looked over the fence on my way to school. The gum wrapper was gone. I stared at the clean spot on the gravel. I looked up at the house. Dark, hollow eyes in the armor stared back at me. That afternoon I let my empty mochi crunch bag fly out of my hands and over the fence. I tried to catch the bag as it floated away. I wanted him to think it was an accident. The next day the bag was gone. And then I knew.

I threw a bottle cap over the fence, an apple core, an empty guava juice can. Those disappeared too, so I knew he was alive, but I began to feel guilty. Maybe I was making him feel bad, making him angry, and he was waiting by the window with a BB gun.

So the next day I carried a white handkerchief tied to a stick and waved it as I ran by and tossed a yellow plumeria over the fence. It was a perfect, fresh plumeria, without any brown streaks, because I'd picked it from the tree, not from the ground. The next day it was gone. I threw a red hibiscus from the schoolyard, a double gardenia from my mother's favorite bush. Then I started in on her orchids: a Dendro-

116

bium, a spray of Vandas, a giant yellow Cattleya. Gone, gone, all of them gone.

The day I flung half a strand of maile leaves over the fence, I thought I heard something. A tinkle at first, and then several tinkles. I looked around, but there was no one. And then I saw them, two spoons and three forks dangling from the mango tree. They hung from one of the inside branches, so you couldn't see them unless you tried, and they banged against each other when the wind blew. I wasn't sure how long they'd been there, because the wind didn't blow as hard where we lived, on the leeward side of the island. It was a Kona wind that day, the kind we got before a storm, the kind that brought ashes when the volcano was erupting on the Big Island.

I wore a white scarf and skipped past his house, not too fast, so I could hear the spoons and forks. I lobbed fruit over the fence, ripe fruit wrapped in paper towels and placed in brown paper bags to cushion the fall. A papaya from our yard, a small Chinese banana from Aunty Hannah Mele's house, wild guava from the old Pali road, mountain apples and dates from Nuuanu. More spoons and forks, then butter knives and measuring cups, an old grater and a colander clinked in the mango tree.

I wrote a haiku about the tiny birds that ate the uncooked rice my mother threw on the driveway. It started out as a sonnet, but I kept scratching out words because I didn't want it to get too personal or he might get the wrong idea. I folded the sheet of paper into an airplane and flew it over the fence. Parts of a chrome fender and metal rods, some long, some short, banged together in a sudden gust.

I sent him the lyrics of a Hawaiian song that my tutu had sung to me over and over again until I learned it by heart. It was a song about missing the cliffs and longing for the rainbow colors of Kauai. Many, many radio dials dangled from wires and beat against old tin cans. I had never paid much attention to the wind before, but now I rejoiced in the gentlest puff.

My whole family could hear the clanging now. We sat on our stone wall and listened to the chimes in Lani's mango tree. "At least he's doing something with that junk," said my father. He sent Buzzy over with an old pair of sheet-metal cutters. "Just leave it by the gate." My mother cut up half a banana cake she'd just baked and told Buzzy to take it over too. They didn't know what I was doing. I had been careful not to let them see.

I told only Ruthie Ito, because I needed her to teach me how to fold origami cranes. I knew how to fold balloons, but I wanted birds, so I swore Ruthie to secrecy. Before we folded the many squares of colored paper, I printed fortunes on the back. "All the troubles you have will soon pass away." "Try a new system or a different approach." "Soon you will be sitting on top of the world." I let a string of cranes fly into Lani's yard. They disappeared, but nothing new hung from the tree, not for a whole week, when I spotted a cluster of rusty silver half-moons and stars twinkling in the dark.

I threw an essay, a page a day for a week, one in which I wrote that statehood was stupid, that we didn't need haoles in Washington telling us what to do. My idea wasn't popular at school and the teacher gave me a C, but I didn't care. I wanted him to know I could think for myself. I wrapped the last page around a kukui nut I'd polished with sandpaper and then oiled until it gleamed. Green copper suns rose in the mango tree, complete with rays welded on.

118

At school I studied the Hawaiian dictionary and created a list. "Lani," I discovered, meant heaven, sky, a very high chief. I tried to remember what Lani Gerard looked like, but all I came up with was a shadow that moved in the dark, an outline I tried to color in. I lay awake in bed at night, listening to the chimes Lani Gerard had made for me, chimes I could never touch, that rang only with the help of the wind. And I thought of more things to send over the fence, things that would mean something, things he could keep.

Whenever Buzzy mowed our lawn, I gathered up a handful of freshly clipped grass. I blessed the grass with the strongest, the best words I knew. Hauʻoli—happy. Hoʻolehua—strong. Maluhia—peace. Aloha. Mana. Lani. Koʻu hoaaloha—my friend. I tossed the grass through the openings in the fence, then watched it fall like rain upon the gravel in Lani Gerard's front yard.

Hawaiian Salt

My mother shows me how to cut fresh pineapple. I am nine years old. I stand at her elbow and watch.

First cut off both ends, then slice down the sides to remove the skin. Cut out the eyes. Now rub the whole pineapple with Hawaiian salt. Otherwise the juice might burn your skin, might burn your mouth. You only need to rub salt on fresh pineapple. Salt makes the pineapple sweet.

————

Before going back to college in Oregon, I go to the supermarket to buy mochi crunch, cuttlefish, oyster sauce, and Hawaiian salt. A big Hawaiian woman stands in front of the salt. She is reading the label on a white bag.

Sea salt, what kind salt is that? I want Hawaiian salt. Is this the kind? Why don't they have red salt? And why the package say don't eat this kind? Who wants to buy if you cannot eat? Real lolo, if you ask me.

————

Uncle Wing eats sweet Maui onions dipped in chili-pepper water and chunky red salt.

Gotta have Hawaiian salt or no taste ono. Gotta have Hawaiian salt for poke, for kalua pig, everything. The other kind salt no more taste, good for nothing except baking cake, and who wants to eat cake, not me. Me, I like everything salty. Hot and salty. Good for drink beer.

———

The woman in the supermarket holds the bag of salt next to her ear and shakes.

All my life I eat Hawaiian salt, and now them guys tell me it's no good. They should come Hawaii. Try my poke and my huli huli chicken. Bet you they don't have good kind poke in Washington, D.C. I don't like it when they say our salt no good. Just like it's poison. Look how big I am. Do I look like I'm dying? How they expect me to wash the salt? What you think you get in the end?

———

Aunty Hannah Mele is out on the lanai making lau lau for the poi supper. Poi suppers are just for family. Not as many people or as much work as a luau, and we eat lau lau instead of kalua pig. My aunty cuts fresh pork butt into chunks and places the meat on luau leaves. She sends me to the kitchen to get some salt.

Make sure you get the Hawaiian salt, not the haole kind. Hawaiian salt taste more ono because of all the fish, all the seaweed soaked up.

———

The Hawaiian woman points at the row of blue car-
tons—the ones decorated with girls holding umbrellas.

Who going eat all that junk kind salt? All the taste, all
the ocean, all the Hawaii wash out. Why they gotta make
our salt like that?

Pick Up Your Pine

Aunty Hannah Mele got me the job in the pineapple cannery this summer. She got me the job because she has pull. Connections, pull, at least twenty years of pull—first as a packer, then as a trimmer, and now as forelady on one of the lines. Just tell the boss you're my niece, she said. Tell him you're fast. Tell him you're good.

Pineapple ripening red and gold in the fields, pineapple waiting to be picked. Waiting for the pickers to snap off their crowns. Crowns off and pineapples rolling onto the belts, into the trucks. Rolling, poking and shoving with thorny skins, out of my way, out of my way. Pineapple ripe and rolling onto the belts, into the trucks, poking and shoving their way to the cannery in town, near the wharf.

———

I wait for the 5:30 bus in front of the mama-san, papa-san store down by the highway that goes into town. My jeans rustle as I pace in front of the store in the cool morning air. My jeans are stiff and very blue, and I have to roll up the cuffs four times. Even though it's still dark, papa-san has already opened the store. I long to buy something from the crackseed rack—a bag of cherry seed or red coconut balls. Something sweet to add to my lunch. My mother has packed me a bologna sandwich on brown Love's bread and a Red Delicious apple. But I haven't earned any money yet, and the bus pulls up, the inside lights still on. I sit in the front, close to the driver. I press my face against the glass, watch for my stop, the building with the giant pineapple sitting on top.

Pineapple coming in from the fields, poking and shoving, and smelling ripe. The smell of ripe pineapple filling the air, falling thick and warm as a blanket. When the bus stops at the cannery, I can smell where I am.

Aunty Hannah Mele waves at me as I walk past her line. See you lunchtime, she says. She is one of my Hawaiian aunties, married to my goong goong's youngest brother. A tall, regal woman with long hair piled on her head like a crown. If not for the hairnet holding down her hair, I know it would glow. Girls, she says to the women sitting on stools, this is my niece Mahealani. Mahi, say hello. But these are not girls. Many of them are as old as she is, older than my mother, way older than me.

———

The whistle blows. Six-thirty. The boy feeds pine one by one to the genaka machine. The girls check him out. They shout, Oh da cute, but he cannot hear them. Oh da cute kine guy, our genaka boy is cuter than the others. Pineapple falling out of the genaka, pineapple rolling down the line, where the girls are shouting, where the girls are singing. Our pine is sweeter, our line is faster, the best in the whole cannery, no ka oi, no ka oi. Pineapple marching one by one down the line where the trimmers and packers wait. Pineapple with their cores removed and their skins chopped off. Pineapple already looking like cans.

I am a trimmer, and I will earn a nickel more than the packers. I'm not on Aunty Hannah Mele's line. I'm on my own and have my own forelady. She sees my red badge. Red instead of white, so she knows, so everybody knows, I am a child laborer, not yet sixteen.

Pineapples marching in front of me now. I sit at the front of the line, where the pine falls out of the genaka machine. Pick up your pine, pick up your pine, the forelady shouts, as the trimmers trim and the packers pack. The trimmers trim the eyes still staring from the pine, eyes that the genaka has missed, eyes that must not go in the cans. Roll the pineapple around on your thumb. Then make diagonal slashes across the pine with your knife. See the eyes fall out, four, five at a time. See how fast, that's what you want. No time to cut out one eye at a time. Then put the pineapple back on the line. Pick up your pine, pick up your pine.

You have to catch every one of the pine. Cut off the eyes before they get away. Cannot let even one slip by. So roll the pine faster on your thumb until your thumb muscle aches, and you see it swell and you see it grow and you wonder if your muscle will burst. Only half an hour has gone by and your thumb is already sore. One week sore, one month sore, sore and swelling, sore and aching, when will it stop? When will it stop?

The women next to me are singing, but I don't know the words. I can hear only the chopping of the genakas and the grinding of the belts and the clanking of the cans. And the forelady shouts from behind, Pick up your pine, pick up your pine. Other hands reach for the pine, but not mine. I am trying to spin a whole pineapple on my thumb. The forelady yells, paces up and down, finally yanks me from my stool at the front of the line and moves me to the end of the row of trimmers. She points at a plastic tub. She makes the words big in her mouth: Fill. It. Up. I remove pineapples from the belt that the trimmers have missed because they are one girl short, because of me. I grab the pineapples before they reach the slicing machine. Haul them to the front of the line where the faster trimmers trim. Eyes left and right flying off the pine. The girls are singing, knife blades flashing, and I am catching pine.

Pineapple twirling on thumbs, knives slashing, eyes falling into the trough, cans and belts clattering, banging. And the marching, pineapples marching down the line, from the trimmers to the slicing machine, from the slicer to the packers, from the packers to the cans. And all the way down the line, the forelady cries, Pick up your pine, pick up your pine.

The forelady pulls me from the line again. The whole line moves up a seat, including one of the packers. I move to the front of the line of packers. Next to the machine where the slices fall out. What about my extra nickel an hour? Are they going to pay me as a packer or a trimmer? A dollar quarter doesn't feel as good as a dollar thirty, but now I have to pick up only three or four slices of pine at a time. Neat, beautiful Life Saver slices, falling like fresh bread out of the bag. Looking even less like pineapples and more like cans now. Twelve or more slices at a time. Slices to admire, to toss into cans waiting on trays. Trays that the tray boys haul away.

But first you must decide. See the dark yellow slices,

the translucent yellow, those are number one. All the rest are number two or three. If really bad, then number three, but try not to have number three. See the white flecks, the solid yellow. No flecks in number one, so this is two. Two not as sweet, but still good. Three is the worst, so you don't want three. Not as good money as one and two. Good lines have more number one. Number one is the best, no ka oi, no ka oi.

I stand at the best place in the line of packers. At the front, first in line, where I can scoop up all the number ones. I can pick up ones all day, smile, think how beautiful, how sweet the cans I've packed. Next time we go to the store I'll know how to look for the number-one cans. But the forelady yells at me, Pick up the rest! Pick them all up! The first four slices are easy, but not the ones that follow.

Pick up your pine, pick up your pine, the forelady shouts, and the trimmers trim and the packers pack and their lips mouth the words of the music trying to drown out the genaka machines. Knife blades flash to the beat, cans bang in the trays, and the pineapples march down the line, down the line.

Why have I never noticed ones and twos before? What if I put a two in a one can or a three in a two can? If a one goes in with a two, will they know? If a three becomes a two and a two becomes a one, then which is really a two, which is really a one? How do you know? How do you know?

The packer next to me on the line picks up all the slices I miss. She packs faster than I can think, and her cans fill up with number ones. Twos and threes evaporate. She sees what I cannot see fast enough. The forelady yanks me from where I am frozen, sticks me at the end of the line again, gives me a plastic tub. Points. I know. I pick up the slices the packers can't pack in time. Catch them before they fall into the trough and go where the trimmings go, to the juice, to the juice. To the juice, and what a waste of good pine.

Stop the line? Never happen. Never heard of such thing. Not this line, not my line. The forelady grabs the tub from me, and she and the first packer empty out the bin. Slices fly out of their hands and into the cans. Number one, number two. Number two, number three. Number one, so easy; number two, just like breathing.

Pick up your pine, pick up your pine, and don't get juice on your arms, don't get juice in your eyes. The juice can make your skin break. The juice can make your skin bleed, and you will have to go to the infirmary, and the nurse will wrap your arms in gauze, long strips of gauze, and everyone will know you were careless. Get juice in your eyes and she'll call an ambulance. The juice can make you blind. This is no joke, this is no joke.

A splash on my arm. A small squirt of juice. No, no, not me, but I show the forelady. Hold out my arm like it's diseased, not mine. She points to the infirmary, and the pine keeps rolling and the slices keep flying, and the nurse washes off my arm with lots and lots of soap and water. I don't see blood, I am lucky this time, but you can't take a chance. I stare at my arm, at the inch of raw skin turning pink, turning red. Is it the blood churning below? Is it the blood waiting to flow? Just one square inch of pink on my arm, and the nurse wraps my whole forearm in six inches of gauze. Six! All the way up to my elbow. Did you get any juice on the other one too? I shake my head no. But she checks, sees a little pink, wraps that one up too, just in case, just in case. But no juice in my eyes, so back to the line.

Back to the line, but I can't pack now. Can't pack, can't trim, too slow, can't get close to the pine with gauze on both arms, so the forelady makes me sweep. Get the broom, sweep the floor, let them see who you are. Let them see the gauze, see the badge. A red badge because still fifteen, a red badge and white gauze, gauze that hides blood. No more trimming and packing today for you. One arm wrapped in gauze is bad enough, but two. Two means you have to sweep the floor and everybody knows who you are.

The whistle blows. Eleven. Half an hour for lunch and only a half day gone. I spend ten minutes walking quickly to the locker room, taking off my gloves, washing my hands, using the toilet. I will need ten minutes to powder my hands and put the gloves back on. That leaves me ten minutes to eat. So walk fast to the cafeteria, where Aunty Hannah Mele sits. Waiting for me. She holds out a frosty can of guava juice. Oh, you got hurt, poor thing, but no worry, you will be okay, come and sit by me. You want a bite of my tuna fish? She gives me a piece of kulolo she has steamed the night before. She knows it's my favorite. She gives me some to eat now, some wrapped in foil to put in my locker and take home. I bite off chunks of the chewy taro pudding, savor the sweet taste of coconut milk.

After lunch the forelady sends me up the ladder. I climb way up, way above the packers and the trimmers, above the conveyor belts and genakas. I climb up the ladder and crawl across the catwalk over to the big chute. Everything that falls into the troughs passes through this chute. The pineapple pulp and the pineapple skin, the pineapple cores and the pineapple eyes, all the trimmings, all of it falling, falling out of the chute. Falling so fast I cannot see what is what. My job is to catch the knives, the knives that fall in the trough. The knives in this mess? The knives falling fast? But how can I see them? How can I catch them? Look for the blades, look for the shiny part of the knives. Catch them before they fall into the juice, before they jam up the machine and the whole cannery has to shut down, shut down. Grab them by the handle, not the blade, or you'll get cut and your fingers, your hands might fall into the juice, into the juice. Sit and watch everything falling, everything flying, and try not to think about what you heard at lunch about the boy whose arm got caught in the genaka machine. Where did the arm go? Into the trough? Into the chute? Did it get in the juice? Don't miss, don't catch the knife wrong or they will have to stop the lines and close the place down because of you, because of you. And who knows what will happen to the juice, all of it turning red. Red, po ho, what a waste.

I catch two knives. Two, by the handle. Two very smart very fast good eyes saved the juice. Saved the juice. Everything is falling, flying by, and I see it all and I do not see anything. I do not see what I am seeing, and my eyes are so tired, and I am so dizzy, and how did I catch them? How did the knives get up here? How did *I* get up here? I'm afraid I will fall into the pulp, fall into the juice. Where is the forelady, why doesn't she come? Everybody down there, working the line, will they forget about me up here? My head banging, my body shaking, and the whole cannery rushes by, rushes by.

———

The whistle blows. Three o'clock. Pau work. Silence except for rubber gloves snapping, feet shuffling, the girls saying goodbye. A kiss from Aunty Hannah Mele as I walk past her line. A kiss on my stink face. Don't worry about the arms. You'll be better tomorrow. So stink and the bus is already crowded and who wants to stand next to me. Not me. Stink and tired and hot and I want to sit down, lie down and go to sleep and never get up. Don't want to touch anybody. Don't want them to smell me, so hauna, so hauna. People get on the bus at every stop. They sit down, then stand up for anyone older than them. When one gets up and one sits down, all the people standing on the bus have to move. Move to the back, move to the back, the bus driver yells. Some people get off, some move to the front, some move to the back. Sit down, stand up, all the way home. I know they can smell the pineapple on me, on my clothes. Overripe pineapple, rotting in the sun. My jeans are no longer stiff, my cuffs unroll, shirt sticks to my back. The gauze itches my skin, and I want to scratch, scratch, scratch it all off.

Long walk up the hill in the afternoon sun. Take a bath, eat, fall into bed at eight. Pineapples still marching across the lawn, pineapples walking on the stone wall, fingers, legs falling into perfect slices on my plate. The forelady shouting, Pick up your pine, pick up your pine. I give up my seat on the bus to number one.

No pineapple in my fruit cocktail. This pineapple isn't ripe. Can't you see the yellow is wrong? No pineapple juice for me. Rub it with salt before you eat. No pineapple on my pizza. Wash your mouth, wash your hands before they bleed. No pineapple in my mai tai. No piña colada, please.

Ocean Is for Drowning

My friends from the mainland make fun of me. They swim out to the reef and shout at me to join them. They laugh when I shake my head. They expect me to swim like a fish because I am Hawaiian. They think all Hawaiians can swim.

I haven't told them my uncles threw me off a reef when I was five. Uncle Joey laughed when he told me about this. He said that's how they taught kids to swim in the old days. All I remember is the big wave at Sandy Beach, the one that dragged me in when I was seven. The wave picked me up and slammed me down. Sand and water got in my nose and mouth and I couldn't breathe. I didn't know which way was up. Uncle Joey pulled me out. That was the second time I almost drowned.

Now when I go to the beach with my friends, I swim in shallow water and watch them dive off the reef. And when I go with Buzzy to Sandy Beach, I stay on the sand while he bodysurfs with his friends.

"Don't do it," I tell Buzzy. "You know what happened to Roy."

Buzzy hasn't seen Ruthie Ito's cousin Roy. Roy used to be a champion swimmer, but he broke his neck body-surfing. He almost made the Olympic team. He had a job all lined up as a swimming coach after graduating from the University of Hawaii. But just before school started, Roy went bodysurfing on Maui. When Roy didn't stand up after the fourth wave hit, Ruthie's brother dragged him out. I went with Ruthie to visit Roy. He lay flat on his back and blinked his eyes at us. Roy's sister told us that a lot of people have broken their necks at Makena, but nobody puts up a warning sign, because the hotels don't want to scare away the tourists.

I told Buzzy about Roy.

"He just lies there. He can't even get up and go to the bathroom."

"That's the breaks," said Buzzy. "All my friends go to Sandy Beach. You can't stop me, so shut up already."

———

I begged my mother to let me take synchronized-swimming lessons at the YWCA. I wanted to swim like Esther Williams, because she swam with her head above-water. But I couldn't glide across the pool without splashing. I couldn't do somersaults or dolphin flips or make my arms look like shark fins. I couldn't swim across the bottom of the pool without coming up gasping for air. I had forgotten how much time Esther Williams spent *under* the water. The teacher made me leave the class and go back to the beginners.

———

When I go to the beach with my family, it isn't hard to avoid the water. Unlike my friends from the mainland, my family goes to the beach to catch fish and eat and camp out, not to swim. Uncle Joey dives for squid and octopus, Buzzy snorkels on the reef, but they are the only ones who go way out. My father, Kuhio, drinks beer with the other uncles. He used to swim and surf when he was younger, but he doesn't anymore. The kids play in the tidepools formed by the coral. The rest of us sit in the shade of the tents and play cards. My mother brings all the food from the freezer and cupboard that has been sitting around for too long and needs to be eaten up. We eat potato chips with clam dip, See's candy, dried aku. We play what-the-hell, go fish, and trumps. My father buries a bucket in the sand and puts up a canvas wall so we don't have to run all the way to the public toilet. We don't swim laps. We splash water at each other. We don't race out to the reef. We lie on scratchy army blankets and joke and talk story until Uncle Joey and Buzzy bring in the fish. We spend our time beside the ocean, not in it.

———

I swim in the green water, the shallow water without coral. I try to remember what I have learned about breathing in air and blowing out bubbles. I like the breaststroke, because I can line up my chin with the surface of the water and don't need to stick my head under. I don't swim out too far, because I know it's just me and the ocean in the end. Whether I'm sitting on the sand or swimming near the shore, I never stop thinking about drowning.

It's easy for my mainland friends to laugh. It's easy for people like Buzzy and my uncle, who already know how to swim. They've gone out and come back safe. Like Esther Williams, they can smile and relax in the water. They are not stuck in a groove, like Roy, like me, playing the same wave over and over again.

Huhu

"Buzzy's huhu," said Benjie as soon as my mother and I walked into the house. He didn't even give us a chance to set down our shopping bags before he greeted us with the news. He lay sprawled on the couch in shorts and a white T-shirt, watching a rerun of *Sea Hunt* on TV and eating popcorn mixed with dried cuttlefish.

"Buzzy's huhu, Buzzy's huhu," repeated Nani, jumping up from the floor and running over to us. "See? He kicked a hole in the door." She wiggled her fingers through a tear in the lower part of the screen.

My mother shook her head. "What's he mad about now?" she asked as she walked into the kitchen and opened the freezer. She planned to fix roast duck from San Francisco Chinatown for supper, Buzzy's favorite, and she'd forgotten to thaw out the duck before we went to Ala Moana. My father liked to eat by six, so if supper wasn't ready by then, Buzzy wasn't the only one who would be huhu.

"Cops caught him and Kumu stealing pineapple for the luau," said Benjie. On the tube Benjie's idol, Mike Nelson, swam through a jagged opening in the side of a barnacle-encrusted ship. My brother gnawed a strand of cuttlefish as he spoke. "And then Dad got him classified 4-F."

My mother dropped the frozen duck on the counter.

"What?" She walked into the living room and stood between Benjie and the TV. "Did you say 4-F?"

"Yeah, Dr. Chong wrote a letter. Told them Buzzy has a bum back." Benjie stretched his neck so he could see what his hero had found inside the ship.

"So he doesn't have to fight!" shouted Nani.

"This better be true," my mother said. She looked confused, afraid to be happy, in case they'd got the story wrong. Perhaps she was angry too. All those months of argument and now my father had gone ahead and done what he wanted without telling her first. She walked over to the television and turned it off. Benjie groaned. "What did Buzzy say? And where's your father?"

"Dad's on the lanai, with Mi Nei," said Benjie. "Buzzy didn't say nothing. He just took off."

"He took the pickup," said Nani.

"What's this about cops?" I asked.

"Cops caught them, but they didn't have to go to jail," said Nani.

"Dad told him go pick pineapple for the luau," said Benjie. "Couldn't get sweet kind at the store. So him and Kumu went Wahiawa side to pick."

"And they got fined fifty bucks," added Nani.

"What?" said my mother.

"Daddy's huhu too. He keeps saying 'no son of mine.' "

"Oh no," said my mother. I groaned too. It was going to be a long evening.

"Where did Buzzy go?" I asked Benjie.

He shrugged. "He said he's not coming back."

"Not coming back?" said my mother.

"He says now he can't coach at Kam."

"Are we still going to have the luau?" asked Nani. "Who's going to help Daddy with the pig?"

"I can," said Benjie. He sat upright now. "I can catch the pig."

"No, you can't," said Nani. "You're too small."

"Look who's talking small," said Benjie.

"Enough, you guys," I said. My mother was already headed for the lanai.

———

My father had promised Buzzy a luau on the beach. No ordinary party for my older brother's graduation from Waipahu High. We had a birthday to celebrate too. Buzzy turned eighteen on the first of June.

"We can have a luau just like the old days," my father had said to Buzzy. "Hula girls, ukuleles. On the beach. Waimanalo, maybe Lanikai. You can spear some octopus. Maybe we can use the net. A real hukilau."

My father and Uncle Wing sprouted the idea on Easter night, late, while watering themselves with highballs. The other uncles, aunties, and cousins had already gone home after gathering at our house for an egghunt, potluck, and an evening of playing cards.

"Don't listen to them," my mother warned Buzzy, as if we didn't already know my father often forgot promises made while he'd been drinking. But the next day, as he peeled Easter eggs and ate them dipped in Hawaiian salt and chili-pepper water, my father raised the subject again.

"I'm telling you, Anna, it's real easy for do. We can roast the pig at home and then take it over to the windward side in the pickup. We can shred it and salt it and leave the bones at home."

"But you can't take pig up the Pali. You know it's bad luck."

"Won't go over the Pali. We can take Likelike Highway through the Wilson Tunnel."

"How are you going to keep the pig hot?" asked my mother.

"Just throw the tarp over it. Buzzy can drive faster than the cops."

"Sure, and what about the rest of the food?"

"We can cook it here too, and maybe some at You Jook's house. Everybody can help. We can camp out afterwards."

"What about the haupia? What about the beer? How are you going to keep everything cold?"

"What about, what about. I tell you, Anna, you worry too much." He turned to Buzzy. "And you can invite all your friends."

"All of them? You mean my whole class?"

"Sure, why not?"

"But there are almost two hundred."

"So we roast two pigs."

"Oh no," said my mother. "Not two pigs. You're not going to dig up my papaya tree."

"Just your good friends," said my father.

"Only one pig. I mean it, Kuhio."

"Then we can do it?" Buzzy asked my mother.

"Sure," said my father.

"We'll see," she said.

Out on the lanai my father slouched on a chair he'd carved out of a stump of koa wood. He held a bottle of Jim Beam in one hand and clasped our bulldog, Mi Nei, by the neck with the other. He said Mi Nei reminded him of Goong Goong. Mi Nei didn't have Fook's face, but she had his legs, squat but strong, and most of all, she had his personality. "Tough buggah," but wouldn't hurt a flea.

"No son of mine," my father muttered to Mi Nei. He tugged her jowls, and she growled. "I told him, Doc, get him off."

"What's going on, Kuhio?" asked my mother. "Did you really get Buzzy out of the draft?"

My father's eyes were half shut already and yellow tears caked in the corners of his eyes. "Tell Buzzy, not me. Doc got him off."

"Dr. Chong helped you?"

"Yeah, Chong. Good guy. Boat went away. Without my boy. Now Buzzy huhu with me."

"Why didn't you tell me?" She kept her voice low, so Benjie and Nani couldn't hear, but I could sense the complaint in her voice.

"What? You like him die?"

"No," she said. "Of course I don't want him to die." I waited for her next words, *But I should have been there.* Tell him, Ma, I thought to myself. *I could have made it better.* But the words never came. She tugged Mi Nei out of his grasp and pried the bottle out of his hand.

"Go inside the house," she said to me. "Start the rice."

My mother didn't cry until after Buzzy called to say

he wasn't coming home for supper. He was going to stay at Kumu's house for a while.

"Don't be mad at your father," she told Buzzy on the phone. "He's only thinking of your own good."

After she hung up, she said, "He says he'll be home for the luau. He needs time to cool off. Just as well." She spoke as if trying to convince herself.

"What about graduation?" I asked. "Who's going to help Dad?"

"I don't know, Sister," she said. "I just don't know."

She put the duck back in the freezer and went into the bedroom and shut the door. When she came out, her eyes were swollen. She fixed canned corned beef, watercress salad, and rice for supper and said we could have extra scoops of chocolate ice cream. She even let us watch TV while we ate. My father wouldn't come in the house, so she took a couple of plates out to the lanai and sat with him until he ate.

————

Maybe it was just as well Buzzy wasn't home to see how relieved she was. Whenever Buzzy and my father argued about the draft or signing up, my mother avoided taking sides. She tried to stop them from quarreling, but if she couldn't, she left the room, just tuned out. I began to think maybe she thought Buzzy would avoid the draft in the end, since one of Uncle Danny's war buddies sat on the draft board. My cousin Frankel had gotten a deferment, and so had Beetle and Bobby Michelangelo. Why fight an unnecessary battle?

But maybe there were other reasons for her silence, ones I knew she would never admit. That she wanted Buzzy to escape. To go into the service so he could get away from home, get away from my father. That she didn't want to think about war. That if she worried about Buzzy dying, it would certainly happen.

I remember the night an air-raid siren went off in our back yard. By accident, I suppose, since we didn't get hit by a tidal wave or a hurricane. No enemy planes flew overhead. No bombs fell. My mother came to my room to check on me. The loud, whining blare of the siren had jarred me awake, and I was standing on my bed, peering through the glass louvers, looking toward Pearl Harbor. I was waiting for the sky to light up in the grand finale, like my teacher Mr. Chen had promised. The Bomb that would take us all.

"What are you doing?" she asked.

I smiled. I was so happy to see her. She looked like an angel, dressed in her white nightgown.

"Are you dead too?" I replied. "Are we in heaven?"

"Go back to sleep," she said. Her face was pale in the moonlight. She tucked me in, rubbed my brow with her damp, chilly hands.

Not long after that I read about Vietnam in the *Star Bulletin*. We weren't at war yet, but I felt it coming. That summer my mother went to California for a long visit with Aunty Lucy and Uncle Chin. She took Benjie and Nani with her. I stayed home and cooked for my father and Buzzy. They didn't like what I fixed, so my father took us to Scotty's Drive-In for hamburgers every evening after supper. I was so depressed, I didn't sew any clothes for school that coming fall. I was convinced we would never see September. When my mother asked, I said I didn't need any new dresses; the old ones still fit. I knew I couldn't tell her the truth.

Buzzy told me he'd pick the Marines when the time came, that he might not wait for the draft.

"I can swim and dive better than all them guys," he said. "I want to help our country, Sis. I can do it. They need me."

"Don't do it," I pleaded. "Listen to Dad this time. He's right. You're just being hard head because he says no." It was the wrong thing to say, of course, but how could I tell him I was afraid?

My father wanted Buzzy to go into business with him. Buzzy would get a degree in business administration, and they'd set up a shop where my father could sell his paintings and carvings along with other art objects. Some imports too, and knickknacks better than the crap the tourists were getting in Waikiki. Buzzy could manage the store, keep the books. My father even knew of a good, inexpensive place to rent on Kuhio Avenue, and he would hang on to his job at Pearl until they started making money.

"No way!" yelled Buzzy. "Ma can do the books. I'm not sitting in a shop like some old fut." My brother wanted to teach P.E. and coach. Swimming, track, football, you name it.

"Your Goong Goong had a shop," my father replied.

"Forget about Pop," my mother interrupted.

"Stay out of this, Anna." Turning to Buzzy, he said, "The place will be yours when I'm gone. This will get you started."

My mother got up from the table and walked into the kitchen.

"I don't need your help," said Buzzy. "I can go to the U.H. on the GI Bill when I get out."

My brother had always wanted to go to Kamehameha,

the school for Hawaiians and part-Hawaiians in Kalihi. But at first my parents couldn't afford to send him, and then Kam tightened up on admissions. Buzzy went to the Kam School games—football, basketball, as many as he could get to, hitchhiking if necessary. He knew the players' names, sang their alma mater after the games.

"Kam School, Kam School. That's all you can think," yelled my father. "What makes you think they want you?" Buzzy flinched at this. He stomped out of the house and slammed the door.

Buzzy scored high on the SAT, but by the time graduation approached, his GPA had fallen from 3.2 to 1.9. He didn't apply for college. Not even the U.H. Instead, he lined up a job as a lifeguard in Waikiki. He started working weekends right away and planned to go full-time after graduation.

"You can't do this," my father shouted. "You can't be a beach bum for the rest of your life."

"Why not?" said Buzzy. "You were one. You and Fook."

"Don't talk like that about your grandfather."

"I don't even remember him."

"He can't help it he died so young. Is that what you want? You want them to draft you?"

"Maybe I'll sign up! Anything to get away from you!"

"Enough, enough." My mother finally interfered, but she couldn't stop their arguments. It took the promise of a luau on the beach.

———

We talked about the luau every night for three weeks, until we'd worked the whole thing out. Almost. The plans kept changing as we came up with better ideas. Sometimes our own, sometimes suggestions made by Uncle Wing or Uncle Joey or whoever dropped by. For every obstacle my mother raised, my father and the rest of us came up with a solution. Buzzy and my father stayed up late, drawing up more and more elaborate plans. Regular and contingency plans, so nothing could go wrong.

So what if none of our relatives had a house on the beach where we could throw a luau. Who needed a house? Hawaiians camped out on the beach all summer. Our family camped every year on the Fourth of July. This time we'd go a little earlier. We'd pitch the tents on the beach the night before Buzzy's graduation. The next morning we'd throw the pig in the imu first thing, go to the graduation ceremony, then head for the beach. We'd prepare the rest of the luau food ahead of time and cook soyu chicken feet in large kettles on outdoor grills for the people who showed up at the beach early.

"Piece of cake," my father kept saying.

After seeing how cheerful Buzzy was, how he and my father were seeing eye to eye for a change, even my mother got into it. She called the neighbors and asked them to save orchids and plumeria and ferns. She asked a Portuguese guy at work if his son's band could play. Aunty Hannah Mele and her troupe could entertain with Hawaiian music and hula dancers, but my mother knew Buzzy and his friends would want some rock-and-roll.

But she made my father promise. "Just a small luau."

"Right," he said. "Just one, maybe two hundred."

"And not everybody staying overnight."

"Right. Just the family and the people close." He winked at Buzzy.

Buzzy crooned as he washed the dishes. I could tell

how excited he was, because he put the milk in the cupboard and his dirty clothes in the garbage can. Every day after school he was out in the yard, mowing, weeding, or watering plants. Everyone he invited accepted. Many of his friends had family parties to attend first, but they planned to end up at ours.

"Plenty good-looking guys coming," he said to me. "Why don't you ask some of your cute girl friends. We can dance on the beach. We can even go swimming in the moonlight." He raised his eyebrows twice and grinned.

———

The house was so quiet with Buzzy gone. I lay in my bed, listening to my father mumbling in a low voice. He was talking to the painting on the wall again. "No worry, Fook," I heard him say. "Buzzy no go. My boy stay home."

I missed Buzzy, missed the way he filled the house. Even when he was angry, at least you knew he was there, you always knew where he stood. He didn't know how to shut up and lay low. He always had to be right, even when being right caused other people grief.

I thought of the time Buzzy was lead dancer in the dragon dance in Chinatown on Chinese New Year's. Drums beat and firecrackers exploded as the dragon wound its way through the crowd. My father carried Nani on his shoulders, and she screamed as the dragon's mouth came close, as if trying to bite off her head.

"Don't worry," my father said. "It's only Buzzy inside the head." But Nani started crying. "It's for good luck," said my father. He pretended to lunge at the dragon.

"Don't make him mad," my mother said.

I focused on the legs, telling myself this was only my

brother holding up the head, but in black pants and white sneakers, his legs looked like all the others in his kung fu club who held up the dragon's body and tail. The red and gold eyes and gaping mouth reached for me next.

"Give him some money," my mother said, shoving a dollar into my hand.

I stuck the bill into the dragon's mouth, and the arms inside raised the head high, then tossed and rattled it back and forth.

"Quit it, Buzzy," I shouted. "Don't!" But the dragon kept tossing its head, and the drums beat faster. "Why doesn't it go away?" I looked to my mother for help. She stuffed a five-dollar bill into the mouth, and the dragon, and my brother, finally turned away.

"Terrific dragon," said my father. "Best one I've seen."

Later that evening I told Buzzy he should tell Nani he had been inside the dragon's head, that it was all make-believe, so she could sleep.

"Me?" he said. "Not me. That was a real dragon." Then he roared and leaped around the living room until Nani cried and my mother said stop.

———

My mother finally brought up the luau the next morning. "Should we call it off?" she asked my father.

"Hell no," my father said. "Who needs him?" He grabbed Mi Nei's leash and headed down the driveway. The neighbors said later they saw him fall off the curb, but they couldn't see how. He just fell. Hit his head on a parked car, broke his ankle, and passed out.

In the hospital he told my mother, "I don't remember what happened. And I wasn't even drinking."

"You hit your head," she said. "Doctor said to watch you in case you have a concussion."

"Concussion!"

"I know what that is," said Nani. "I saw it on TV. The guy went foam at the mouth."

"Daddy's not going to foam," said my mother. "You and Benjie go out in the lobby and play."

When they were gone, my father said, "Maybe I have a brain tumor. I was just walking and then I don't know. I must have blacked out. You know what happened to Fook. Better tell the doctor to X-ray my head." He looked very pale.

"They already X-rayed."

"And?"

"You don't have a tumor," said my mother. "You just fell down." But when we arrived at home, she got on the phone and started dialing. First Kumu's house, but there was no answer. Then the aunties and uncles.

"You seen Buzzy?" she said on the phone. "Kuhio fell down and Buzzy's luau is next week. What am I going to do? That's what I said. Fell and broke his ankle. Right. Cracked the bone. He might have to have an operation. And he might have a concussion. You're telling me oh no. Who's going to do the pig? Who's going to dig the imu? Who's going to do everything? Sure, I know everybody can help, but Buzzy's not even home. Yeah, he took off. He and Kuhio had a fight. He doesn't want to be 4-F. I'll tell you later. It's a long story. He even got caught stealing pineapple."

Each call took a very long time, because she had so much to explain. But by the fifth call, she'd found him. Or at least located someone who'd seen him. Aunty Ah Oi said Beetle had seen Buzzy the night before in Waikiki. At the Outrigger Hotel. With a girl.

"What girl?" Pause. "A haole? From the mainland? What do you mean, Beetle could only say hi. Because of who? He was with his in-laws! Oh no." When she finally hung up, she said to me, "Ah Oi said Beetle said the girl was hanging all over Buzzy." She opened the refrigerator and peered into it, trying to remember what she was looking for. Then she opened the freezer, and the duck from the night before fell out. She threw it back in and sat down at the counter.

"Oh, Buzzy, Buzzy." She rubbed her temples with her fingers.

"He probably went to work," I told her. It was Sunday. "What if we go to Waikiki and look for him?"

———

But instead of Buzzy, Kumu sat high up on the lifeguard stand at Queen's Surf. He grinned down at us.

"Ay, howzit, Mrs. Wong. Mahi."

"Have you seen Buzzy?" I shouted.

"Buzzy no stay," said Kumu. "Told me cover for him little while." I was relieved to know my brother wouldn't run off and let people drown.

"But why?" my mother asked. "Where is he?"

Kumu shrugged and turned his palms up, but I could tell by the way his eyebrows unfurled that he knew something.

"Heard you guys got caught stealing pineapple," I said.

"Yeah," said Kumu. Big smile. He slouched forward

in his chair. "Fifty-dollar pineapple! Twenty-five bucks for one stinking pine! Lucky thing we only pick two. Buzzy went give me da kine money for pay. Otherwise I be jail. So now I go pay him back."

"They know you covering for him?" I asked.

"Nah. No need." He pulled his straw hat down over his eyes. "Lousy buggah never even let us keep the pineapple. Told us throw them back." He slapped his thigh and shook his head.

"You know about the 4-F?" I asked.

"Yeah. I tell you, man, Buzzy real huhu. I told him, Why? You lucky. I wish my father try for get me out."

"Kuhio fell down," said my mother. "He broke his ankle. He might have to have an operation."

"What? Father fell down? Buzzy never tell me that."

"Buzzy doesn't know," said my mother.

"Ho, man." Kumu shook his head. "Big trouble, hah?"

"Yup," I said. "And there's the luau too. You know where he went? Come on, Kumu, you better tell." I stared him right in the eye. He looked away, out at the water, as if he wished someone would start drowning and save him from tattling on his best friend.

"He went Maui," Kumu said finally. "Buzzy went Maui."

"Maui?" shouted my mother.

"Yup."

"What for?"

He shrugged.

"What I told you, Kumu," I said. "No fool around."

"With my sister's friend from the mainland. Nice haole girl. From Iowa, Chicago, someplace like that. Ay, not what you think. She stay older than him. Came with the college choir. All them guys went. Buzzy went too. Tour guide." He grinned. "Listen, when I pau work I come help you guys, okay? Call up my friends come too. Mrs. Wong? Mrs. Wong?"

———

Fortunately, my father didn't foam at the mouth and didn't need an operation. The break was only a hairline fracture after all. But they wrapped his leg in a cast that rose above his knee and gave him a pair of crutches. The doctor told him to keep his foot raised so it didn't swell. No alcohol either, because of the pain pills. If the ankle didn't heal by itself, they would go in and pin it together.

"No way!" my father said. "No nails in my foot!"

My mother said, "Better call off the luau," but my father wouldn't budge.

"No look good," he said to her. Besides, we weren't even sure who was coming, and those who were had probably already invited *their* friends, Hawaiian style. Plus we'd ordered and paid for the pig and already started fixing the food. We couldn't let all that food go to waste. After all, Buzzy had said he was coming, and he wouldn't lie about that, would he?

While my father sulked in front of the TV with his foot on the hassock and a pile of pillows, my mother lined up extra help. I counted. Five uncles, four cousins, and three of Buzzy's friends, plus Kumu—thirteen men and boys to stand in for my father nursing a lame leg and my brother playing tour guide on Maui. One of the uncles offered to lend us his truck. Uncle Joey, Kumu, and Beetle would haul the pig from the slaughterhouse while Uncle Danny, Benjie, and the others fired up the imu. Some of the uncles on the windward side would pitch the tents, and some of the aunties would go out early to cook the chicken feet. Others would show up at our house to help with the rest of the food.

"Who needs him?" my father said again when he heard who was pitching in to help. He was feeling good, smiling. "Who needs Buzzy? Everybody ohana. Everybody kokua."

———

At dawn on graduation day, my father lay on a wooden lawn chair in the back yard with his leg in a sling held up by a rope looped around a steel cable that was hooked to the garage post and the fence in back. Uncle Wing had rigged the cable so the uncles could carry my father back and forth across the yard without having to untie his leg. They lashed him to the chair so he wouldn't roll off. He barked out orders through a megaphone that Nani had made out of construction paper.

"One more rock in the leg," he shouted, as the uncles shoved the red-hot lava rocks into the pig's cavity. The rocks sizzled and steamed as they seared the raw pink flesh.

———

When Buzzy entered the stadium in his cap and gown later that morning, we waved our arms and shouted, "Buzzy! Buzzy! Over here!" We sat in the front row of the bleachers so we could make a quick getaway after the ceremony. Buzzy heard us and waved.

I turned to my father. "Look, he sees us." But my father was squinting off into the distance, as if trying to see something across the field. His crutches lay on the step behind him, and he had pulled my mother's muumuu across his leg, over his cast. I was surprised he did that. Surely Kumu had told Buzzy about my father's foot. Didn't my father want Buzzy to feel sorry for him? It occurred to me that my father might actually be enjoying the attention. Still, I wondered why Buzzy hadn't called. Were things that bad? Didn't Buzzy care?

When Buzzy walked across the stage between Albert Wong and Winifred Woo, we cheered. Buzzy tossed his diploma in the air and caught it as he leaped off the stage.

"That's my boy," my father said, clapping long after the rest of us had calmed down. He wiped the sweat off his face, but didn't complain once about his foot, even when the uncles jogged him back to the car right after Buzzy received his diploma. We raced out of the stadium to beat the crowd. I looked around as we ran, hoping Buzzy would catch up with us, but all I saw were the graduates cheering, whistling, their caps and tassels flying through the air.

———

We were eating the chicken feet when Buzzy and the haole girl arrived at the beach. My father lay on the lawn chair with his foot sling attached to a cable that ran the full length of the big tent. Uncle Wing had improved the system by placing the chair on a wooden platform with wheels. He and the other uncles had laid out a path of sheet metal and pulleys so my father could haul himself back and forth across the sand. Benjie and some of the cousins were trying to see how many chicken feet they could eat without breaking up the bones. They tossed the mangled feet twenty feet away into a washtub half buried in the sand.

A chicken foot with claws still dangling landed at the

girl's feet as she and Buzzy approached the tent. She jumped back and screamed, "Oh my God!" It wasn't a high, weakling screech but more like a roar, the deep, thrilling kind. An alto, for sure, I thought. Everyone stopped eating and talking and looked up. Chicken feet swung in our hands, chicken feet hung half in, half out of our mouths. Piles of bones lay everywhere.

"Look, Ma!" Benjie shouted.

"Buzzy! Buzzy's here!"

My mother ran up and hugged him. He held his body stiff.

"Your hands are sticky," he said.

"You made us so worried," she said.

"I'm okay, Ma. I told you not to worry." His voice broke as he spoke. He cracked his knuckles, something he does when he's trying to act tough. His eyes roamed the tent until they fell on my father, who sat on the far side of the tent with a pot of chicken feet on his lap.

"And who is this?" my mother said, turning to the girl. "Aren't you going to introduce?"

"This is Elsa. Elsa Olman. She's Norwegian. I mean, her parents are. She's from Idaho. She lives on a farm, with chickens and all."

"Iowa," said Elsa. "How do you do?"

"Chee, big girl, hah?" said one of the aunties. "I never knew Norwegian girls was so big."

"Shhh," I said. I was sure Elsa had heard, but she smiled nonetheless. She towered over my mother, almost Buzzy's height. She didn't look at all like the girl I pictured hanging all over my brother. He and Kumu had bragged about the blondes and the redheads who came on to them in Waikiki. Coeds squeezed into tight shorts and halter tops, shapely girls. Elsa wore a white eyelet blouse and a yellow calico skirt. Her short brown hair rose off her neck in small waves. Her nose was a little on the big side, but then so were her eyes. Big eyes, as green as a warm ocean.

"Hi, I'm Mahi, Buzzy's sister. Glad you could make it." I handed Buzzy an orchid lei. "Here," I said to him. "You give it to her."

"Thanks, Sis." He gave me a grateful look. I nudged him toward her.

He dropped the lei around her neck and pecked her on the cheek.

"No, kiss her on the lips!" Nani shouted. Buzzy finally cracked a smile. He complied. Elsa blushed.

Buzzy turned to me. "Elsa likes to sew," he said. "Like you and Ma."

"That's nice," my mother and I said at the same time.

"Isn't it?" said Elsa. The three of us laughed. Buzzy looked puzzled at first, then joined in.

"Introduce your friend around," said my mother. "And then you better go talk to your father."

As Buzzy and Elsa Olman walked through the tent, the buzz of voices started up again. The buzz and the chewing, the buzz and the gnawing and spitting out of bones.

"Who is she?"

"I heard they went Maui."

"Maybe she can sing for us."

"Buzzy no look *that* mad."

Buzzy moved from table to table, saying to Elsa, "This is my aunty. This is my uncle. This is my aunty. This is my uncle." I followed behind. Elsa whispered to Buzzy at one point, "What are their names? Are they really all related to you? What am I supposed to call them?"

"Just call them aunty and uncle," he said. "I forget all the names."

They finally made their way to my father, who must have been the only one in the tent who wasn't acting as if the Pope had arrived.

"You okay, Dad?" said Buzzy. He nodded at my father's leg.

I waited for my father to yell. I longed for him to break the silence that held them apart. To my surprise, he said, "No sweat. All taken care of. So who's your friend?" He held out a chicken foot.

As relieved as I was, I confess I felt a pang of jealousy. Elsa didn't look embarrassed or guilty, which is how I would have felt if I had been gallivanting around Maui with somebody's son while that somebody was laid up with a broken ankle. I didn't know what Buzzy had told her about my father or the draft. I still hadn't heard his side of the story, and I wasn't at all certain that I would.

———

My father said they must have brought her up right in Iowa, because she sat right down and ate three chicken feet, even though Buzzy said she didn't have to eat any if she didn't want to.

"Don't be silly," she said to Buzzy. "I've cleaned pigs and milked cows."

My mother kept fussing over them, bringing them something to drink, people to meet. I knew she was glad, relieved like me. Buzzy was back, he wasn't going to war, and fireworks hadn't gone off in front of all these people. "Save room for the luau," she said. "We have lots more food coming."

Buzzy jumped up. "I better go help."

"No worry, sit down," said my father. "We got it covered. All you gotta do is smile and eat."

"But who's gonna bring the pig from the house?"

"Same guys that caught 'em."

"Who dug the imu?"

"Uncle them. Get plenty help."

"Yeah, Buzzy, no worry," yelled Kumu from a nearby table. "We go pick up the pig little while." He held up his thumb and baby finger and waved a shaka as he spoke. Other shakas went up too. "No worry, no worry."

Buzzy looked around the tent. His eyes were red. His arm shot straight up in an unmoving yet unmistakable shaka. "Thanks," he said. "Thanks, everybody."

Elsa said, "I can't wait to see this pig."

"Bet you don't have pig like this in Iowa," said my father. "You go back, you can tell them how." He launched into a graphic description of the roasting of the kalua pig.

———

My mother cried when Buzzy got up and danced the hula later that night. He took off his shirt and tucked some ti leaves into his shorts. A maile lei draped his neck and chest. I poked some ferns into my haku lei and put it on his head. He gave me a hug. I clung to him for as long as I could, until my father said, Hurry up. Aunty Hannah Mele sang and her musicians played while Buzzy rolled his hips in a comic, hapa haole hula. We laughed and clapped. Some of the men whistled. Then my father chanted while Buzzy danced a song of ancient Hawaii, a warrior's song. A cool breeze from the ocean blew through the tent, and all we could hear were the waves crashing and my father's singular, haunting voice. Buzzy did not smile. He slapped his chest and his arms and his thighs and kicked his heels until the sand flew. And from his throat came grunts, shouts, and a deep, low rumble, like a dog growling at the moon.

I Never Saw the Volcano

I never saw the volcano, but I could tell. I told Kuhio, See the ashes falling like big black petals from the sky. They floated all the way from the Big Island on the Kona wind. The ashes turned Nani's diapers black, so I had to wash them over and over again, and then I still had to shake them out. The couch turned black, and the floor and the beds and tables too. The whole sky smelled like barbecue. It was so hot I couldn't sleep. I could tell it wasn't sugar cane burning, because the ashes were so big and they fell all over, not just by our house, but even in town, at Popo's house. I could tell it wasn't just leaves burning. It was whole trees. Houses. Even my cousin's house on the Big Island was burning. A brand-new house. Right in the middle of the volcano path. And their furniture, even her cedar chest from Hong Kong, all burned up, just like that. I told her not to buy that house, but he said, Can't beat the price. Can't beat the price because you know why.

Fee simple land is not easy to find, that's why they had to go to the Big Island to buy. That's why we came to

Pearl City. We're lucky we don't have to lease. The red dirt in our yard gets all over everything, but at least it's ours. If we had to lease, in fifty years they could kick us out, all of a sudden, just like that. Then we wouldn't have a house. We would have nothing, not even dirt.

I never saw the volcano for real, only on TV. You could ride the helicopter over the volcano, but it cost too much, and you might fall in. Kuhio wanted to fly over the volcano, but I told him, Over my dead body. Besides, we needed the money to buy a new couch.

I don't have to see the volcano to know it's real. Everything feels so stuffed up. It's like when you want to throw up and only the dry comes out. You cry because you can't throw up enough. I can tell by the way the ashes hang in the air for a long time before falling down. You can't sleep at night because it doesn't cool down. There are no tradewinds, only hot, dry Kona wind. The ashes are so big and fall all over everything. The diapers never get clean no matter how many times you wash. And you don't know what you're shaking when you shake the diapers off.

Family Shark

I can tell when Fook's ghost might come to visit. The moon is full. The house has finally cooled down, but I can feel a warm breeze blow through the louvers in the living room. Anna is asleep. I can hear her in the bedroom, breathing but not too loud. Thirty years married and she still doesn't snore. I pour two jiggers of Jim Beam, straight up, one for Fook—just in case—and one for me. I sit in my chair in the living room and wait.

———

The first time I met my future father-in-law, Fook, I thought he was a ghost. Like the gui they told me about in China when I was a boy. Or one of the Hawaiian ghosts I heard about from my mama, Puanani, when I came back to Hawaii. I even thought he might be our family aumakua, the shark.

When I first started surfing, my mama used to say, "If you get trouble, Kuhio, you look for the aumakua. The aumakua help you out."

"Sure, Mama," I said.

"It's true," she said. "I saw the aumakua. Two of them. Big white shark. They circle round my brother, but they never went bite. They never go way until his body wash up on the beach. They like make sure we find him before they swim away."

"Okay, Mama," I said, but I listened only with one ear. That's how I made it through all those years in Sun Yin village. Pretending to believe. When my father finally sent for me to come back home, I thought I left all those ghosts and family superstition behind. Just let them float away in the wake of the boat. That was before I heard about the Hawaiian ghosts, before I believed in the aumakua, before I met my future father-in-law, Fook, while moonlight-surfing at Waikiki.

———

I was a beach boy when I met Fook. A beach boy by day, and by night a bellhop, a dishwasher, or a busboy—I did anything the Halekulani paid me to do. Business was good in Waikiki after the war. Lots of honeymooners and retired folks. The hotel needed Chinese-Hawaiian guys like me to smile at the wahines, even the married ones. When I wasn't working, I hung around the beach. I ran on the sand to build up my legs and helped my friend Kimo with his surfboard rental business. I hosed down the boards, checked out the girls, and carried the boards down to the water so Kimo could teach them to surf. I didn't mind that he didn't let me teach. I just liked to be there, on the hot sand, close to the water, out on the waves. I loved the salt air, the palm trees along the shore. Even the tourists didn't bother me. Diamond Head never looked so good. I was very happy to be back home.

———

I got off work at midnight, my usual time. I left my shoes at the hotel and walked barefoot out the side door to the beach. I hated to wear shoes, and the sand felt so good between my toes. The moon was full, second full moon that month. I remember, because on the first full moon I had let Kimo talk me into going moonlight-surfing.

"Nothing like it, brah," he had said. "Just like making it in the moonlight." He closed his eyes and rocked his hips, and the other boys on the beach laughed.

Kimo was right. Surfing at night was better than daytime, because nobody could see me. I lay on my board and floated over the swells. I didn't have to get up on my board. Didn't have to surf. Didn't have to show off and look good for the wahines. That's when I did my best thinking—when I was out there bobbing around. Nobody, nobody could make me do anything. My only problem was the moon. The full moon made me think too much.

———

Chinese people love the full moon, man ngit—always celebrating, eating moon cake, ngit biang, always waiting for man ngit so they can do something when the time is right. After my father left me in China with my grandparents, I counted the moons. I prayed to the full moon to bring my father back.

My father, Khi Fong, was a tall man. He wore a white hat and a white suit and carried a black cane. He didn't use the cane to walk. He used it to touch whatever was in front of him. He tapped the tile roof and the brick wall of my grandfather's house. He poked the mosquito net over the bed. He swatted the flies that landed on the meat. And before he left me, he tapped my shoulder with his cane and said, "You grow up to be a gentleman, Doong Keong." He only called me by my Chinese name. Never Kuhio. He didn't like the name my mama gave me.

I was only five years old. My younger brothers were still babies when my father shanghaied me. My sisters weren't even born. I forgot how everybody looked. I even forgot my mama, Puanani, but I could still remember how she smelled. Like fish and salt. She used to carry me on her back when she picked seaweed on the beach. When she bent down to pick the seaweed, the ocean floated up. And when she stood up, the ocean fell back down. So many nights I dreamt about the ocean. I dreamt that China was an island that kept shrinking and shrinking. The water kept rising and rising, until I could only stand on China with one foot. From Sun Yin village it took about three days by cart to reach the shore. They never let me go to the harbor, because they were afraid I would run away. I didn't see the ocean again until I was eighteen years old. That's when I finally came back home. By then we were at war, and I had to go away and fight. So much time I lost.

————

The beach was quiet at midnight. Just a few servicemen, drunk and singing bad songs. I liked to run home along the edge of the water, toward Diamond Head and then up Kapiolani Boulevard. When I passed by Queen's Surf, I saw my friend Kimo carrying his board down to the beach.

"Ay, brah," he said to me, pointing to the sky. "Second-chance moon. Surf's up. You going out?"

"Nah," I told him. "Just pau work. Gotta go home eat." I dragged my feet a little in the sand so he could see how tired I was, then I turned and headed toward the road. Fast, so I couldn't hear what he said next. I ran past the zoo, past the Ala Wai canal, to my parents' house. I had only been back one year when my father died. After that, I shared the house with my mama and my youngest sister. It was a big house, three stories tall, with many bedrooms. My mama left on the lights to scare away the ghosts. First thing when I came home, I checked all the empty rooms.

"Sometimes I hear his cane," she said.

I didn't sleep real good at night. Especially when the moon was full.

———

After I ate the stew and rice my mama left on the stove, I took out my brush and ink and rice paper. I rubbed my ink stick in the well until the water grew black and thick enough for the brush. When I couldn't sleep, I painted. I learned to paint in China as part of my studies to become a gentleman. I learned to speak and write in Mandarin and hakka. I learned to carve ivory and wood and paint in watercolor.

My favorite was painting jagged mountain peaks. And bamboo with all the joints and stalks bending to show which way the wind blew. Bamboo and mountains were easy, so I usually started with them. But not that night.

First, I painted a peach tree with a trunk full of knots, and then branches and leaves. The peaches were ripe and plump and practically falling off the tree. Beneath the tree

I drew a woman holding a peach in her hand. I painted her eyes, almost closed, looking down at the peach, her hand raised, and her mouth, open just a little, ready to take a bite. But when I finished, I realized she wasn't like the women my teacher in China taught me to paint. Her eyes made a frown, and her lips curled into a dragon's mouth.

I knew at once who she was. My aunty in China, the only one who didn't laugh and hug my father and me when we got off the boat. I had nightmares about her. I dreamt she didn't have a body, just a face. Many faces, paper thin. Her faces flew around me like birds, and they shouted, "Ngar man fan choi nai town? Ngar jook choi nai town?" Where is my dinner? Where is my jook?

All those years I lived in China, she cooked for us— my father's parents, her daughter, me, and all the aunties, uncles, and cousins who came to visit. She stayed in the kitchen while we ate and only came out to bring us more rice or another bowl of pickled cabbage when my grandfather rapped his chopsticks on his plate. My father talked to everyone except her, but I saw him go to her bed the night before he left. The next day she didn't go to the ship with the others. She was the one who stayed home with me, and she was the one who held me down when I found out my father wasn't coming back. Her hands were cold and bony, but she was very strong. That was the only time I heard her laugh. "Ki-ki-ki-ki." Like an angry bird. She laughed and cried and rocked me back and forth until I couldn't cry anymore. I didn't find out the truth until I was fifteen, when my aunty's daughter told me that my father was her father too. Somebody had to stay home and take care of my grandfather and grandmother. I didn't hear her laugh except that one time.

My parents' house felt hot and damp, even though the windows were open. Sweat ran down my neck, and I was more awake now than before. I checked all the rooms again. My mama was still sleeping. She never had any trouble that way. Then I decided to go back to the beach to cool off.

I kept my surfboard at Kimo's rental shack. When I got there, Kimo's board was back in its place. I thought maybe the surf had gone back down, and that was okay with me. Kimo said I could use any of his boards, but I liked my own. I was so proud of that board. I carved it from our old front door. I had to put lots of varnish on it so it wouldn't get waterlogged and sink. It was heavy, but I knew it could hold me up.

I threw my board in the water and paddled out. Past Queen's Surf, past Cunha, and before I knew it, I was way out, all the way to Castle Point. I heard about the big ones at Castle Point, but I had never gone out that far.

It was just me and the ocean. Me and the moon.

Trouble was, I could see too much. Even in the dark I could see turtles, dolphins, whales—every kind of beast you can imagine. I felt them under my board, lifting me up and dropping me down. I kept my eyes on the moon and tried hard not to think, tried not to see too many things. I saw white ghosts run across the water and then disappear. Dark shadows circled my board under the water. Could it be a shark? I wondered. Maybe the aumakua my mama told me about?

That's when I saw it. The black shadow flying across the wave. Small but growing bigger, coming straight for me. I heard it scream. And, oh, what a scream. Sounded like half man, half wild pig. Made my heart beat so fast. And then I couldn't see the moon because of the wave. It came up so fast I almost got caught. One second, that's all I had. I dove off my board into the wave. I stayed down as long as I could. It was so black down there. No sun to tell me which way was up.

Seemed like forever when I finally came up. I coughed and choked and I couldn't find my board. I swam around to look, but it was gone. Then another wave hit. And one more after that. That's when I started praying, praying for the aumakua to take me home. I didn't want to get caught in the current. Maybe I would get washed out to open sea, and after that, who knows where I could end up. Maybe China. I thought about my mama, who didn't know where I was. I didn't want her to lose me again. My father was only one year passed away, so she needed me even more. That's when I said to myself, Kuhio, you better swim like hell.

I could see lights on the beach. How far away they were. I was a strong swimmer, but the current kept pulling me out. That's when I heard him. Not the scream again, but a man's voice. I suddenly realized he was scolding me in hakka, my very own dialect.

"Ngee hei mang nge ma! Ngee hei so gai ma!"

I wondered, How can the aumakua speak hakka? Who was this calling me stupid and blind? Then I thought maybe he was a Chinese ghost, the gui, coming to take me back to China. Maybe he was the gui of my ah bak goong, who died without telling the family where he hid the gold he found in California. My grandfather said my uncle's ghost could not sleep until he told someone.

"Maybe he's waiting for you, Doong Keong," he said. "Maybe you will be the one he can trust."

Not me. I didn't want to be the one. Thirteen years I spent in China, trying not to let my uncle's ghost catch me, and now he had found me in Hawaii. Out in the ocean. Without my surfboard.

The voice came again, this time shouting in pidgin, "Gunfunit, man, you like this damn board or what? I not going bring in two boards myself."

I thought for a moment it was the ghost of my father, but my father spoke only good English when he spoke it at all, and I had never heard him swear.

My surfboard flew at me, right out of the dark. I cannot tell you how good that old door felt. I climbed on and started paddling.

Not my uncle, not my father, not the aumakua. Then who? I didn't plan to stick around and find out. Of course, I didn't know it was Fook. He wasn't my father-in-law yet, and I didn't know for sure he wasn't a ghost.

My grandfather in China taught me always to treat the gui with respect. So I shouted in my best Mandarin to the dark shadow drifting away, "Excuse me, dear venerable ghost. It was not my intention to get in your way. The ocean belongs to honorable spirits like you. Forgive this poor, innocent man who was caught in the spell of the full moon."

But Fook didn't speak Mandarin. Besides, he was now getting smashed by a wave which I had distracted him from.

I decided I'd better get lost fast. So I caught the next swell without even thinking. Man, I never knew I could surf like that. It was the wave I had been waiting for all my life, my longest ride up until then. When I finally ran out of wave, I fell down. And when I came up, there he was. Fook. Right next to me, sitting on his board.

"Aiiyaa!" I screamed. Oh, he made me so scared.

"You fresh off the boat or what?" he yelled.

It was a miracle—when I think about how big the ocean is and how small we are, and yet I kept on bumping into him like that. Three times, if you count the shadow and the voice and the man.

"Sorry ay, brah," I said. Then in hakka, "Ngai e wui ngee hei gui." I thought you were a ghost. I wanted him to see I was pake like him. Sure, he was mad, but he didn't look big enough to beat me up.

"Gui?" he said. "You thought I was gui? Auuuweee!" He slapped the water and shouted in hakka and pidgin *and* Hawaiian. "You almost drowned, you lousy, good-for-nothing pake. Lucky for you I came along."

——

He laughed all the way up the beach. Worse yet, the next day all the guys on the beach heard about me. To this day, when I run into one of my old surfing buddies playing cards or shooting pool, he says to me, "Remember the time you thought Fook was one ghost and he got so mad he almost broke your surfboard in half?" Sometimes they said he broke my board. Sometimes he broke my face. I never knew what the story was going to be, but I knew who was going to come out ahead in the end.

He was a small man, not tall like my father, but much stronger and quite a rascal. He lifted barbells and ran on the sand with fishing weights tied around his legs. He never wore a shirt when he was on the beach, so everybody could see his muscles.

Once Kimo asked me, "Did Fook tell you he learned to surf from the Duke?"

"What Duke?"

"The only Duke. Duke Kahanamoku. No joke."

Can you believe? Duke Kahanamoku, the king of surfing, taught the little pake, my father-in-law, Choy Wah Fook, how to surf!

But Fook didn't talk about the Duke. Maybe he wanted me to think he always knew how, and I was too chicken to ask. But after that night, I saw Fook all the time. When he saw me on the water, he waved at me to stick by him. He didn't let me just ride the swells.

"Now," he shouted. "Go now!" And I went. I did whatever he told me to do. He knew just how long it took me to get up on my board and paddle to catch the wave at the right time. He taught me to tell the difference between the waves. "Just like sleeping with a woman," he said. "Never the same, but you think it is."

Kimo began to let me teach the haole girls how to surf. He saved the best-looking ones for himself, but the leftovers weren't that bad. We taught only the wahines, not the men. The servicemen, who thought they knew it all— we gave them the oldest, most beat-up boards and sent them way out, beyond Papa Nui, all by themselves. And then we forgot all about them until they washed up on shore. Sure it was mean. But it was real lolo too, because we got paid back in the end when we had to chase after the boards. Fook used to paddle the canoe with me. He told me jokes all the way out, until I stopped feeling sorry for myself. And then we took turns surfing the boards back in.

Fook cried when I gave him the painting of the woman. He said, "What I told you? Cannot make a true pake out of a typical kanaka." He wouldn't listen when I talked about being shanghaied, but he always reminded me about my Hawaiian blood. "You the Hawaiian," he used to say. "You got no excuse for surfing more lousy than me."

Fook hung my painting in his shop on Kalakaua Avenue, behind the high chairs where the servicemen sat while he polished their shoes. I felt a little bad at first, because I thought if he really liked my painting, he would hang it up at home. But whenever I walked into his shop, even if there were customers around, I usually caught him talking to the woman I painted for him. He'd see me and point at the wall.

"This wahine told me you been drinking too much."

"You should talk," I'd tell him. "I saw you snoring in the corner with your mouth catching flies." All Waikiki could hear him laugh.

I carved him some ivory dolphins too. Real small ones, jumping in the waves. He took those home. Anna said he kept them over his bed.

I had met Anna when she came in to look after the cash register while Fook and I were surfing. I walked into the shop in my slippers and shorts and saw her standing behind the counter wearing a dress, high heels, and an orchid corsage.

"This my business daughter," said Fook. "She study San Francisco. You watch out. She take over the shop someday."

"Oh, Pop," she said. I thought she looked too fancy

for me, but then I heard her crack her chewing gum. And when she smiled, I could see she had her father's dimples. Like little exclamation points.

———

I didn't even try to paint the eyes the way I learned in China. Almost shut, looking only at the peach. I got the eyes from my mama, Puanani—Hawaiian eyes, big and brown. From Anna I got the nose, her cute little pug, and her lips, soft, at that time never complaining. The long, wavy hair I borrowed from her sister Nona. I painted her after I met the whole family, after I fell in love with Anna.

Fook called her the "shark lady" when the wahines weren't around. "Betta watch out for da shark lady," he used to say. And "The shark lady told me you been up to no good." He liked to kid around, even after I married Anna. But I heard him make my mother-in-law promise not to sell the painting.

"When I die," he told her, "give my painting back to Kuhio."

"You're not going to die," she said.

That's how he was, always insisting when something was going to happen. Five years, that's all the time I knew him. Not even as long as my own father.

———

Even in the dark, I can see her. The moon shines through the picture window on the shark lady. She is mine again now that Fook is gone. She hangs on my living-room wall and can see and hear everything that goes on. I can tell her anything. See how straight and tall she stands, even though the bamboo leans into the wind. She smiles at me, and her head turns to one side as if she is listening. As if she is waiting for him to speak.

Fifty-Dollar Pineapple

Sorry, Sis, this is the only pineapple I could find for you to take back to the mainland. These days, hard for get sweet pineapple. The store kind is sour, not ripe enough. Wish I could pick them from the field like we used to. But you know what happened last time. When Kumu and me got fined fifty bucks. I'll never forget, because it was the same day Dad got me off, 4-F. Kumu tried to pay me back, but I never like take his money. Not his fault. He was only helping me out.

I should have known it was too easy. Thought I was just going to drive up, pick the pineapple, and come home. Cop was waiting right in the field. Just like somebody told him, Hey, watch out, Buzzy Wong is coming to steal.

Every time I think something is easy, turns out I'm wrong. Same thing happened when I went to Lanai to pick pineapple my junior year. I didn't tell you everything. It wasn't all good fun.

That was the first time I ever been in jail. Last time too, I hope. I didn't tell you, didn't tell nobody. I knew if

Dad found out, I wouldn't hear the end of it. I was scared he wouldn't let me go away again. I never told you about the convict too. Oh, lots of things I never told.

Pineapple is a funny thing. Everybody wants their pineapple sweet. Just like me, I'm fussy too. People come Hawaii, they expect to get three things: sun, warm water, and sweet pineapple. You take it for granted. It's when you don't have it that you start to worry. Then you have to ask, Where did it go?

———

I never used to think about pineapple until I worked in the fields. It wasn't easy, out there in the fields. The pineapple company owners just pay the money. The workers are the ones who have to stoop. Sure, get machine, get truck, get everything. But still, somebody gotta pick the pine. Somebody gotta bend down. Somebody gotta knock off the crown and throw the pineapple on the belt. That somebody was me.

Try hold one whole pineapple in your hand all day long. Not easy, especially with the skin still on. So try two. One in each hand. That's how my muscles got so big. First time I picked, I had to hold the pineapple with two hands, just like an old lady. By the end of the day, one pineapple felt like a ton of bricks. I finally got good by the end of the summer. Man, I could flip two pineapples at a time, one in each hand. I could knock the crown off with a bang, right onto the belt. It was tough, but the regular workers did it all the time, even Woody Akina, and he was old, Dad's age, almost bolohead. Didn't talk much, but Woody could flip pine faster than me, faster than anybody. I never could catch up with him.

You had to be tough. You had to be strong. You had to be able to jump for the truck boom every time a tree came along. You know where the pineapple grows is up in the valley where still get trees. The tree grows right up in the middle of the row, and you gotta hang from the boom to get around. You can't go sideways, because the pineapple grows so high and the bush is too poky. Besides, somebody stay in the next row already. When the tree comes along, you gotta jump, catch the boom, so the truck driver gives you a ride up and over the tree. Unless you want to get left behind.

Flipping pine built up my muscles real good. But I didn't think it was so hot at the time. Not when I had to do it day in and day out. But that's not the part that got me down. I mean, it wasn't bad in the field. I worked at night, so it wasn't hot all the time. At dinner we ate potluck style, sitting on the ground. Everything taste real ono when you working so hard. We used to eat pineapple for dessert. All the pineapple we wanted, and I tell you, we earned it. Fifty-dollar pineapple is cheap. We ate the small one, the apple pineapple. They're not the young ones, like most people think. Funny how the pineapple shrinks as the plant grows old.

I ate so much pineapple I got sick. Couldn't eat pineapple for a long time after that. First time was at my graduation luau. Now I only eat it if it's sweet.

Pineapple, pineapple. All that pineapple made us hard up. Had to get our kicks from stupid things. Like, there was no lua in the field, so when you had to go, you had to go right there. The girls climbed over the hill to go. Not real cute-kind girls, not what you think. But after a while they all looked good. Kumu and me and the other guys used to run after them and peek. That's what I mean by hard up.

Even when we were off work we didn't go out. There was a soda fountain place, but the wahines looked too tough for us. That was the whole trouble. No TV, couldn't drive around, no place to shop or go looking for girls. All we did was hang around the dorm, play cards, shoot the bull, just like a bunch of old hens. One time Kumu was lying on the bunk and a knife got stuck in the knothole above his head. We ran outside and saw the other guys throwing knives at the wall. Nothing else to do.

Mostly we sat around, listening to the ex-convict. This was the guy who just got out of Oahu Prison. Man, the kind stories he told! He was in for armed robbery, but that was nothing. He told us about drugs. He told us about what it was like in jail. He talked about his wahine too. This haole chick who used to shoot him up with heroin. He even showed us the marks. And he told us about the sex he had with her. You should have seen Kumu sitting there, panting, like he couldn't get enough.

The ex-convict tried to make friends with me, and I thought, Sure, why not? You gotta give a guy a break. Besides, he wasn't that bad. Just everybody thought he was the one who stole the money the time we all went to the carnival. The rides weren't that good, but the food made me homesick. I never thought saimin could taste so good. Somebody stole our money while we were away, and they all blamed it on the convict guy. They wanted to lock him up. I said to them, Hey, prove it. How you like to be that guy? How you like somebody blame you if you not the one?

Me, I know what it was like. I found out when the

cops threw me in jail and I had to spend the night. I made Kumu promise not to tell anybody back home. I didn't want Dad to sue them or something. It was just a mistake.

I was out jogging. Trying to get in shape for football that fall. Turns out some guy broke into the police station and messed the place up. Real lolo, if you ask me. So then they saw me running, and I fit the description. I guess the neighbors or somebody saw the guy. They thought it was me. Threw me in jail. I tried to argue, but they told me, Shut up. I was in jail one whole night before they let me go. That gave me plenty time to think.

Remember how you wrote to me? And I told you, Don't expect me to write back. I wish I had, but you know me. But every time I got your letter I was so glad. At least I had something. Some guys got nothing the whole time I was there.

When I was in jail, I thought about how so much was luck. It could have been Kumu stuck in there, not me. It could have been a whole bunch of other guys. But they were all sleeping. It was just me.

Even when I was working, my brain was still going strong. You get in the rhythm when you pick. And it's like everything is just marching by. Pick the pine, knock off the crown, throw the pine on the belt, eat supper, take a bath, go to sleep, get up. Same thing over and over again, so the brain has to fight.

I told myself to look up. Don't only look down. It's like when you're hanging from the boom, trying not to get caught in the tree. You look down and all those guys aren't even watching. They're too busy flipping pine. That's when you have to laugh and tell yourself, Hey, this ain't so bad. The hard part is getting up, but when you get up there, you can forget how hard. And the coming down part is easy. Just hold your breath and hang on.

On Lanai you could see more stars than you can see here. I used to lie in the field during break and look up. I never saw anything like that before. I thought, This is where I belong.

So many things I missed. Ma's cooking, taking a bath. I mean, ten guys took a shower after work, and that was it. No more hot water. Kumu and me used to unbutton all our clothes and untie our shoelaces in the truck so we could run like hell to the showers before all the hot water was gone. A couple of times we slept on the floor because we got there too late. Didn't want to dirty the sheets. We were so stink.

I missed the family. I missed all my friends. Sure, I had Kumu, but that wasn't enough. I think every guy who was in trouble on Oahu turned up on Lanai that summer. Or they couldn't find a job, like me, so they had to go to Lanai. So many guys all the same, all trying to make it through the season. And me, I was nothing special. I was just one of the workers on the line.

I went to Lanai because I was sick of Dad squawking. I thought I was going make big money, meet some cute outer-island girl, have a good time. I didn't know I was going to work so hard. I didn't know I was going to spend so much time just thinking.

———

Day before we left, the regulars threw a party for us. We put down our bento cans—to share potluck style, like always. We had rice, sausage, fried cabbage, same old stuff. And then the regulars put down their food. Man, I couldn't believe my eyes. They had everything. Fancy sushi, teriyaki chicken, kal bi beef, char siu pork, noodles, fishcake, roast duck. One guy even had sake in his canteen. Oh, we eat up.

I felt real close to them guys that night. The moon was full, so we worked in the moonlight. By that time I could pick pineapple with my eyes shut. Our line got the biggest bonus for the summer. The luna was real happy. Shook my hand and said, Come work for me next year, too.

When came time for pau work, I didn't want to go back to the dorm. I don't know why. I just wanted to sleep out there. I told myself, Who needs a bath anyway? Who needs a bed? The moon looked good for a while after everybody left, but then I felt the spiders. I had to walk all the way back in the dark. I was pretty tired next day.

Before we left, I went fishing one last time. By myself. I hitched a ride down to Manele Bay and ran into Woody Akina on the dock. He took me out in his boat. Man, I caught a twenty-five-pound ulua that day. Kumu didn't believe, because I gave the fish to Woody. How was I going to cook it? Kumu and me never caught a fish the whole time there, so I didn't think I was going to catch one. Kind of broke my heart, because it was the biggest ulua I ever caught, but Woody was happy. Slapped me on the back and told me next time come stay with him. He said he had four daughters, one my age! I said, Sure, thanks, but the whole way back to the dorm, I was shaking my head.

We took the cheap flight home. Not the real plane. Kumu found us a better deal. One of those single-engine jobs. Just the pilot and his boxer dog up front. Me and Kumu in the back, sitting on the mail bags. When we landed on Oahu, the ground never felt so good.

When I got home, I found out I'd missed the surfboard rental job. You should have told me. I couldn't believe nobody told me. I guess it's my fault for not telling the whole story. But it wasn't really that bad on Lanai. Not the whole time. Looking back, I'm not sorry. Sometimes when I was working in the field, I thought, What am I doing here? Stuck on this rock? But then I thought about how this was only pineapple. There was still everything back home.

I could never be like you, Sis. I can never go away from here. I don't care if I never eat sweet pineapple again. But everything else I'm going to keep. They can't charge me fifty dollars for the beach and the sun and the surf. Hawaii no ka oi, that's what I say. Nobody can make me pay for that.

Monk's Food and Doughnuts

Popo is dead, so the monks are wailing. They march around her open casket beating drums and chanting. They are Buddhist monks from the temple at Nuuanu. They have bald heads and wear long robes. Popo's children do not know enough Chinese to understand what the monks are singing, but they know their mother would be glad.

Popo loved loud music. She listened to the Chinese opera singers on the radio every day. She turned the radio up loud, so loud her grandchildren had to run outside to get away from the noise. Even now the grandchildren listen and squirm in their seats. They like the drums, but not the nagging voices of the monks.

Popo's daughters listen to the monks and cry. The daughters wear white, the color of the dead. The daughters wear white dresses and the sons wear navy-blue suits. The sons stand silent on one side of the casket, while the daughters sit and cry on the other side. Nobody can hear the daughters crying because of the whining of the monks and the beating of the drums. Nobody can hear the crying because of the monks and the drums and the people talking in the hall next door.

On the other side of the glass sliding doors that divide the chapel from the hall next door Popo's friends and relatives eat doughnuts and talk. They eat sugar doughnuts, maple bars, and Long Johns. They eat chocolate doughnuts and cake doughnuts and drink dark, oily coffee, and they talk very loud. They talk about when they saw each other last. Whose funeral was it? Or was it a cousin's wedding? They would rather see each other at a wedding, that's for sure. They talk and laugh so loud they don't hear the monks next door. They don't hear the daughters crying next to the open casket. But that's okay, they are good friends, they're family, and they have come to pay their last respects.

Popo would be glad to see her friends and family eating doughnuts, drinking coffee, and talking. She would be glad to hear them laughing while there was so much crying and wailing going on. Popo was hakka, a sturdy woman. She had big feet and spoke very little English. She learned to read and write enough English to pass the citizenship exam. She raised nine children, five boys, four girls, all by herself after Goong Goong died. He was a strong and handsome man, but one day he got sick. Nobody knew he was so sick. What a shock when he passed away so sudden.

When Goong Goong died, he left her with no money. He left her with nine children, a house, and plenty of land. He was a real smart Chinaman, buying land in Waikiki, Diamond Head, and Makaha. He bought the land when it was cheap. Good thing she had the land, so she could send the younger children to college. Good thing she had the land. Too bad she had to sell.

The monks go away at lunchtime. The wailing and the banging stop at last. The organist plays "What a Friend We Have in Jesus." The daughters cry even louder, but maybe they only sound louder because the monks have gone away. The people in the chapel whisper. They did not know she was a Christian. They don't remember seeing her at church. Then they remembered how her oldest boy, Danny, used to sing and play the piano for her. She cried while he played and sang "Danny Boy." She said he was a good boy, and she loved the American songs. He told her she should come to church to hear the organist play. But she couldn't go. She had too much work, so many grand-children to watch. She had no time, not even time to go to the Buddhist temple. But she loved the songs her son played and sang. She told him, "Tell them play me the or-gan when I die."

So the organist plays Popo's favorite songs at the fu-neral. "Onward, Christian Soldiers" and "My Old Ken-tucky Home." And the tenor from the church choir sings. He sings very loud, but still he can't drown out the noise from the hall next door. He's not the right kind of tenor. He's not as good as the tenor on the *Ed Sullivan Show,* the one who could make Popo cry. Nobody in the family could stand the *Ed Sullivan* tenor, but the daughters cry because they know how glad Popo would be if she could hear this tenor sing.

The people in the chapel get up one by one and tiptoe into the hall next door. The monks were loud, but this music puts them to sleep. They didn't know Popo was a

Christian. They didn't know you could be a Buddhist and a Christian too.

The people talk and eat jai, monk's food. The jai contains no meat, just stewed vegetables, roots, and ginkgo nuts. The monks eat jai all the time. The people eat jai only at funerals. They eat jai today because of Popo. They do not eat meat, because if they do, they eat the dead. They eat Popo. But the jai reminds them of her anyway. The jai is cold and slippery and leaves a funny taste in their mouths. The people eat jai and then they eat more doughnuts for dessert. The doughnuts are a little stale, but they feel much better going down.

The people drink cups of hot tea with the jai. They try not to eat too much. They eat only to pass the time. They want to save their appetites for the Chinese dinner after the funeral. They talk about the food they will eat with the family in the restaurant after going to the cemetery. They know the food will be good. Popo would want them to eat good food. She made the best sweet-and-sour spareribs they ever ate. She always cooked too much food, and she wasn't happy unless there were leftovers. The people remember the Mogen David wine she served with every Chinese dinner. The wine was so sweet, nobody could stand it, but they couldn't say no.

Finally, the organist stops playing, the tenor goes home, and the daughters wipe away their tears. The oldest son and daughter go into the hall next door to make sure everyone is invited to the dinner after the funeral. They invite the aunties and uncles, the friends, the Buddhists and Christians, the first and second cousins.

The people who eat jai and doughnuts will go with the family to Popo's favorite restaurant and eat a seven-course

Chinese dinner. They will eat noodles for long life and roast pork for good luck. They will talk and laugh and eat until they forget the slippery jai and the bald-headed monks. They will laugh and eat and talk until they can't remember the organist and the tenor and the songs. They will eat and talk and laugh until the crying stops.

Red Paper

On New Year's Eve, before my mother died, Kuhio told me he wanted another wife. "Not a real one. Just a mistress," he said. "No matter what, Anna, you still be number one." Buzzy was eight, Mahi was six. Benjie was still in my stomach.

"Go ahead, tell me I'm a no-good bastard," said Kuhio. "Tell me to get lost."

"Enough, Kuhio," I said. "You've had enough to drink. Pop would be so mad if he knew how you were acting." My father had been dead for four years, but Kuhio mourned him like his grave was still brown. Even though I shouted at Kuhio, nobody could hear with all the firecrackers going off. The noise started at noon that day and got louder and louder as midnight approached. My brothers, my sisters, all nine of us were home that New Year's Eve. To see Ma, to be together. We didn't have a chance to do this before my father died.

"I miss him," said Kuhio. He cried and slurred his words. He grabbed my arm, tried to pull me down beside him on the stone wall out on the lanai. "Don't you remember, Anna? Don't you remember how good he was to me? He treated me like I was his son."

"Of course I remember," I said. Kuhio pulled me to him, but he leaned back too far. I put my hands on his chest. I was afraid we'd fall over the wall.

"Don't," I said. "The baby." I smelled the whiskey on his breath. His arms went limp and then his knees, and he slid down beside my feet. Such a big man, yet he looked so small. He covered his head, held his knees, and rocked from side to side.

———

Kuhio was always remembering too much. The years in China happened for him like yesterday. When he drank, he talked. He told me, he told the kids, told anybody who was listening everything he could remember about being sent away to China. How his father tapped him with the cane like he was a guide dog, not a son. How he loved his mother so much but never forgave her for letting his father shanghai him. How his aunty was really his stepmother. How he did not believe in ghosts but they kept coming to visit him. He always blamed the women, as if we had caused him all the trouble. As if we had made his father take him away to China. As if we had a say.

I squatted down next to him. "Come inside the house and eat some rice," I said.

He put his head on my shoulder. "If my father can have two wives, why can't I?"

"Go ahead," I said, pushing him away. "Get another wife. I'd like to see her change the sheets when you throw up."

I had no time for another baby. I was still suffering from morning sickness, but worse yet—my mother was dying. The doctor told us he found two lumps in her throat. That was why she had a hard time talking, why she coughed up blood. "It's a rare type of cancer," he said. "Happens mostly to women. Chinese women. But that doesn't mean you will get it. Maybe it will pass you by."

I told Danny, "I want to set off the firecrackers at midnight." He looked surprised. The men usually set off the string of twenty-thousand, not the women. Besides, he knew how scared I was. I'm the one who found the old man up on Pacific Heights the day Pearl Harbor was bombed. I couldn't burn firecrackers after that. All those New Year's Eves and not one. I didn't pick up the punk again until that night when Ma was dying and Kuhio told me he wanted another wife.

————

I'm not the one who wanted to move to the country, but with my father gone, Kuhio didn't want to stay in Waikiki. "Too crowded," he said. "Too many haoles." But haoles had never bothered him before, when he worked at the hotel, when he spent all his free time on the beach, surfing and fooling around. When my father died, Kuhio quit surfing. He left his surfboard behind when we moved to Pearl City. "It's just an old door," he said. "I'll buy a new board after we settle down." I asked Danny to save the board in case Kuhio changed his mind, but he never did, and I didn't bring it up again. I thought maybe he would open a new door now that we'd closed the other one. But no, Kuhio got his foot stuck in there.

The day Kuhio walked into my father's shop I thought

I could finally forget about Sueo. From the very first Kuhio had a way of looking at me, like he was painting a picture and I was going to turn out better than I was. I liked looking way up at him and feeling his muscles. All those days on the beach made him so strong. But he wasn't just another beach boy. He didn't laugh all the time. He didn't joke. He stared into my eyes and listened to every word I said. Like he heard me. Like I made sense.

Up until then I thought the big love of my life was Sueo. Sueo Watanabe, whom I couldn't marry because of the war. Before I left for San Francisco, I went to see him. I had to sneak out. "I have to go away," I told him. "But I'll be back. I'll get my father to change his mind." I tried to hug him, but he wouldn't look at me. His body was so stiff and cold, like something inside him had died. "Don't forget me," I cried.

I guess that's why I married Kuhio, because he didn't look at all like Sueo. Because Pop liked him, so I didn't have to fight. Because I thought he would help me forget, not because I am fickle with my love.

It was Kuhio's painting that showed me how much I could love. Not the pictures he painted but the way he held the brush. All the soft and tender part of him came out of the bristles and stained the rice paper like blood. He let me watch him paint the first night we were together, before we were married. I knew from the way he held the brush that he would love me for a long, long time.

My father is the one who taught Kuhio to drink. "Suck 'em up," my father used to say. "Can't take it with you." My father could drink all night and never show it. But not Kuhio. He couldn't hold his liquor, but he never said no. When my father died, Kuhio stayed up late and drank alone.

I made new covers for the living-room couch so many times. Changed the sheets, scrubbed the floor, never complaining. Always telling myself he did it from love.

———

Mahi was the one who fought back. Couldn't keep her mouth shut. Always talking back. Even that New Year's Eve, when I told her to run inside the house and get a blanket for her father, she wouldn't listen to me. She threw cracker balls on the concrete, popping them all around us, and wouldn't stop until I grabbed her and shook her hard.

"Get inside the house and stay there!" My hands were still shaking. I could hear her crying as I looked for Buzzy. With all the firecrackers going off, I couldn't hear myself scream, but I could hear my girl. I could hear my husband. If I could forget, why couldn't he?

I found Buzzy at the top of the stairs in front of the house. He and his cousins were screaming and jumping and trying to cover their legs. Joey was at the bottom of the stairs, laughing. He had set off a whistle bomb that followed the kids up the stairs.

"Give me that punk," I yelled at him. I yanked the smoking stick out of his hand.

"Take it easy," he said. I gave him a stink look. I didn't have to say a thing. He knew how mad I was.

"Okay," he said. "Okay."

———

I didn't want to study business. I wanted to design clothes. Not just sew, but make them up from scratch. Maybe that's the part of me that fell in love. When I saw the way Kuhio touched his brush to the paper, the part of me that died in the war came alive again. In San Francisco I used to dress up and catch the trolley to the opera house. I stood on the sidewalk and watched the people go inside. Then I'd go back to my apartment and draw everything I could remember, from their hats down to their gloves. I could see a dress hanging on a rack and remember every seam, every dart. But still I studied. Still I got good grades, and my father called me his "business daughter."

Nona should have worked in my father's shop in Waikiki, not me. She's the one with the business head. She's the one who didn't want to get married. I always bugged her about that, just like my brothers and sisters. "I just want you to be happy," I told her. As if all it took was a man.

———

I didn't have to wait for anyone to tell me it was midnight. I could hear the fireworks getting louder and louder, until the noise was like a big white cloud lifting me up. I pulled up the hem of my muumuu and tied a knot. I took off my slippers so I could run. The red paper and unburned firecrackers felt warm and lumpy under my bare feet. Somebody shouted, "Leave your slippers on!" but I pretended I didn't hear. All I heard was my heart, beating so fast. And my baby, Benjie, inside my stomach, kicking.

My brothers had hung the string of firecrackers from the Hayden mango tree out front. The ground under the tree still showed a little grass, but not much. I didn't even have to look at Joey or Danny to see if it was time. I let the white cloud carry me to the fuse, my hand floated up, and I held the punk steady. Not too hard, not forcing, just touching the tip of the burning punk to the three white strings twisted together. I waited until the strings caught fire and then sizzled. Seemed like forever. *For Ma,* I said. *I light these for my mother.*

Nona, or maybe Joey, somebody grabbed my arm. I fell backward, and they dragged me away as the firecrackers exploded, all twenty-thousand—first one, then twenty, then two hundred at one time. It was so beautiful, especially when the bomb went off at the end and the sky turned white. The sky, the tree, our house, everything and everyone. As if we all blew up and turned into smoke. I could hardly breathe. Then Buzzy and Mahi were pulling at me on both sides, and I looked down at the ground. I have never seen it so red. And then all the bombs in the neighborhood started to go off, bang, bang, bang.

"You were one minute early," said Nona afterward. "I tried to signal you, but you didn't look."

No, not too early. Not that night. Already it was too late. My children would lose their popo too. And so soon after their goong goong.

———

Kuhio didn't remember anything the next day. He ate a big bowl of jook for lunch, then ran through the red paper on the lawn with the kids. He carried Mahi piggyback, both of them laughing as if nothing had happened. Buzzy and the cousins gathered up the unburned firecrackers and made piles of gunpowder dust. Joey taught them how to use the dust to blow up the mailbox and tin cans. My mother sat in the yard and fanned herself and smiled. With the sun out, we could see that nobody's yard was covered with as much red paper as ours.

My mother believed in red paper. She scolded us if

we tried to sweep the sidewalk on New Year's Day. "Leave it for good luck," she said. We weren't allowed to clean the house or cook or wash clothes either. "Whatever you do today," she said, "you will do for the rest of the year." So that day, like always, we sat around and ate leftovers and played with the kids and talked story and laughed. My brothers swept the streets clean that night, but they didn't touch the sidewalk or the lawn. We just let the red paper disappear, into the green, into the brown.

Rainbow Shave Ice

Sweat in the hot sun at Sandy Beach. Hold your brother's hand. Look both ways, then run across the street to the shave ice stand. Stand on one foot. Hop to the other. Give the man the money. Ask for a big one, rainbow shave ice. Vanilla blue, strawberry red, green lemon-lime. Hold the cone tight with both hands. Drink through the straw so the ice doesn't float and fall out of the cone. Walk fast, don't run, back across the street.

———

Go to the butcher shop on Vineyard Street. Hold your breath so you can't smell the meat. Feel the cool rush of air from the freezer. See the clear block of ice, like the kind Popo used to buy from the ice factory in Pauoa. Watch the butcher clamp the block in the vise and shave the ice with the hand crank. Breathe through your teeth. See the snow fall into the paper cones. Take yours with sweet azuke beans on the bottom. Banana yellow, watermelon red, white coconut. Breathe again when you go back outside. Sit in the front seat with the car door wide open. Let the melting ice drip through the hole in the bottom of the cone onto the hot asphalt.

———

Line up in front of the general store in Haleiwa. Stand in line with the locals and the haoles. Listen to the people in line rave about the shave ice. Watch what everybody orders. Ask for a large rainbow cone—pink daiquiri, passion orange, brown li hing mui—over vanilla Goody-Goody ice cream. Sit on the bench outside the store. Feel the first cold bite go right up your nose, between your eyes, and die somewhere inside your skull. Watch the tourists in matching aloha shirts and muumuus. Lift the shave ice up close to your face so the locals can see you. Make them real ono. Tell them to try the Goody-Goody. Tilt your head back, tip the cone to get the last swallow of cold juice, the flavors all mixed up. Feel the hot sun pounding through a rainbow in Haleiwa town, on Vineyard Street, at Sandy Beach.

Crackseed

Aunty Nona could tell what kind of seed a person would buy just by looking at them. She never asked. She just presumed. That July morning, when a tired-looking woman, with hair pinned back with bobby pins, dragged a baby stroller and two screaming kids into Sonny Lim's Crackseed Shack, Aunty Nona held out a wooden spoon. On the spoon lay a sweet-and-sour cherry. The woman tucked the moist seed into her mouth and smiled at my aunty gratefully. Then my aunty handed a smooth football-shaped olive to the boy and two baby apple seeds to the girl. The children immediately stopped crying. While the mother wandered from jar to jar, Aunty Nona squatted down and tickled the baby's cheeks. She tugged the baby's toes one by one. "And what does this little piggy want? And this little piggy?" The baby laughed and the mother splurged on a quarter pound of seeds for each of the older children, a half pound for herself, and a bag of fortune cookies which, my aunty whispered, contained especially good fortunes, better than what you would find in the restaurants. When the woman with fat thighs came waddling in carrying an oily brown paper bag and munching on manapua, Aunty Nona greeted her with not one but three samples—a tongful of bright red mango strips, an extra-large sweet whole plum, and a wet, salty li hing mui. The woman bought a pound of each, plus a pound of pickled green peaches, the special bargain of the day.

I watched from behind the counter, trying to figure out how my aunty knew what people would buy. Was it something as simple as the hair? The size of the people? Did thin people like salty and fat people like sweet? Or was it more complicated than that, and thus more difficult for me to learn?

Before I rang up the sales, she introduced me to each of the women. "Mahi's helping out for the summer," she said. "She goes to college on the mainland. Oregon." She squeezed my forearm as she spoke, and the women nodded at me. "Oregon," they repeated. "How nice. How nice."

Of course, I didn't think about Aunty Nona's ability to sell crackseed all summer long. Just on those rare occasions when I was able to stop thinking about Rascal Lang. He was on my mind so much that at times I wished I was working in the pineapple cannery or in another store at Ala Moana where a big sale was going on, so I wouldn't have time to think. I focused on my aunty's selling techniques because I thought there was a solution in it for me. If my aunty could sell crackseed to strangers, then why couldn't I persuade my parents to let me date Rascal Lang more often than once a week? Why couldn't they see that in Oregon I could date all the haoles I wanted, as often as I wanted? And if they didn't like me dating a haole, a local haole at that, then what would happen if I wanted to marry one? Not that I thought about Rascal in that way, but what if I did? What if it came to that?

———

Rascal Lang joined me in front of the Char Siu Kitchen shortly before noon. Since we couldn't see each other at night, we met for lunch four or five times a week, although I could tell it cramped his style. He pretty much had to spend the morning surfing or bodysurfing at Waikiki, rather than going out to the North Shore or wherever the waves were happening. Besides, it was so high school—sitting on a concrete bench holding hands and feeding each other char siu bao or cone sushi, then walking around the shopping center until my lunch hour was up.

"The summer's going to be over before I get to know you," he complained.

"My father found a condom in the gutter on Sunday," I said. "He thinks it's ours."

"Oh no." He groaned.

"I told him it wasn't us."

"I wish." He squeezed me closer.

"He doesn't believe me," I said. "What are we going to do?"

He didn't answer. "You know, Mahi, the guys have been trying to get me to go to Maui. They want to go surfing at Hookipa."

I cringed when he said this. I thought of the haole women with movie star figures whom I'd seen at Kaanapali when I'd visited Maui with my family. I'd watched the guys on the beach, including Buzzy and my father, gawking at those women, and I'd wished somebody would look at me like that, with the same kind of wide-eyed, slack-jawed stare. I began to regret that Rascal didn't have to work during the summer like me. He had way too much free time.

"Why don't you come to Maui with me?" he said. "Take a week off."

"Are you crazy?" I had to laugh. "I don't even know if my parents are going to let me go out with you again."

"Too bad," he said. "Dave's girlfriend, Sachi, is coming. Her folks are on the mainland." He pulled me close to him and stroked my hair.

I wasn't sure what Rascal saw in me. Even though he could have dated a lot of other island girls, especially the most beautiful of all—the hapa haole girls—he'd chosen me, and I didn't have a single drop of exciting blood. Chinese-Hawaiian girls were scarce in Oregon, but not in Honolulu. I didn't want him to go to Maui without me. I was afraid he'd meet someone really exotic and far more interesting than me.

———

I'd wanted a haole or a hapa haole boyfriend for as long as I could remember. Back when Aunty Nona was dating Benny Rapoza, I'd watch her get dressed for a date. Sometimes she let me run the brush through her long, wavy hair. Her hair wasn't fire-engine red like the uncles claimed, but still, I could see flashes of red as she bent over and brushed her hair from the scalp down to the tips. As I lay on her bed, I'd hold my own strands of hair up to the light and search for a hint of red amid the dark brown. My mother said my hair was not exactly black because of my Hawaiian blood. "What about the Portuguese blood?" I asked her.

"You're not Portuguese" was her reply.

"But Uncle Joey said . . ."

"He's only talking story," she interrupted. "Nobody knows for sure."

I stared in the bedroom mirror as Aunty Nona rubbed rouge into her fair cheeks and painted her lips crimson. I looked at us eye for eye, nose for nose, trying to find a part of me that might be, could be Portuguese.

———

Benny Rapoza was a Portuguese-Hawaiian guy my aunty met while bowling. He was tall and not too dark, with curly golden-brown hair. Bronze, my aunty said, as if he'd won a medal. His eyes crinkled when he smiled, and I loved the way he laughed when I gave him riddles to solve. "Don't tell me, don't tell me," he used to say, holding his hands up over his ears, while I danced around him. He never guessed right, and then when I'd shout out the answer, he'd say, "You way too smart for me." He brought us almond cookies in a box and gave my aunty orchid corsages. When she came out of the bedroom in a tight-fitting dress and high heels, he'd let out a long whistle. She had a smaller waist then, which made her okole look even bigger. My mother used to say Nona was shaped like a pear down there, while all the other sisters were apples. I was an apple too.

That's how Benny Rapoza looked at my aunty, like she was some kind of prize-winning fruit. I didn't see other men look at her that way. I knew he saw what the others didn't see because they thought she was a freak. Benny knew, like I did, that my aunty's skin, although not the right color for Chinese, was perfect, unblemished. That her hair, even though too thick and wild, was just the right blend of light and dark. And he wasn't afraid to say out loud, right in front of Popo and everybody, "You're one heck of a good-looking woman, Nona Choy."

I scrutinized Benny Rapoza carefully, trying to decide which parts of him were Portuguese. Was it his mouth, like my uncles said? Was it his hair? But when haoles from the mainland came to the house, I got confused. I knew they weren't Portuguese, yet why the curls, how come the red or brown hair? And what about their mouths, which seemed to me to be just as big as Benny's?

————

The way my uncles told the story, Old Lady Soong, Popo's mah-jongg partner, nearly fainted when she first saw Nona in the crib, just two weeks old. Old Lady Soong ran out and told everybody that Nona wasn't pure Chinese. That Nona's red hair and pale skin were sure signs of the pak gui. From what I gathered, the pak gui, the white ghost, in this case was a Portuguese sailor who had sailed into the port of Macao many years before and somehow mated or otherwise hooked up with a member of Popo's family. Not Popo, of course, but somebody before her. Thus, Popo's big eyes, which you could see in the family portraits if you looked real close. But none of her children got her eyes. They got Goong Goong's slits. That is, all except for Nona.

"Pohtagee," my uncles teased her from early on.

"Pohtagee hair, pohtagee eyes, pohtagee mouth." They said she was like a poi dog, all mixed up. Plus that, when she was small, she couldn't take a joke. She screamed and threw rocks at them. Fought like a pohtagee too. And then, of course, they wouldn't play with her when she was that way. They ran away from her and hid.

I wouldn't have blamed Aunty Nona for being angry at her brothers. I hated when they talked about the way she acted as a child, like they were never going to let her grow up. Aunty Nona still yelled at them now and then, but mostly she laughed it off. Maybe it was just an act, and she really was hurt inside. But instead of playing down her looks, she patted pale powder on her face and painted a thick line of cocoa eyeliner around her hazel eyes, as if to say, "Look at me. I'm just like you said." And she dated guys who were hapa, guys like Benny Rapoza. I admired my aunty for not feeling sorry for herself, yet something wasn't right. I didn't like the way the uncles singled her out, as if she were the only one in the family who was Portuguese, when for that matter we all could have been. Even if they were only talking story, it was mean. I loved the way my aunty looked. I wanted to have skin and hair like her. I wanted to be different like her. I wanted her to belong.

———

I met Rascal at the beginning of the summer, at a party both of us had crashed with friends. I'd been back in the islands for only a day and was in a great mood that night. My friends talked about how I'd changed. About how I'd bleached out. Didn't they have sun in Oregon? About how my hair looked good down to my waist, how I'd lost weight and looked kind of wild. And I didn't use to laugh that much.

We met at the keg, where I pumped him a beer, making sure to spill off the foam. He'd held his arm out next to mine, his very tan with short golden hair all over; mine faded, smooth.

"Look, I'm darker than you," he boasted.

When he told me his name, I said, "Did you know Lang is a Chinese name too?"

He asked me to go out with him the following night. He wanted me to go out with him every night the following week. My parents didn't like this at all. I'd had a few haole and hapa haole friends when I was growing up, boys, but I didn't really date them. We ran around in gangs. Rascal was the first.

I didn't dare tell my parents that he hated the name Roger, that everybody called him Rascal.

"They might get the wrong idea," I warned him. "They might think you're fast."

———

I didn't know he'd show up at my house for our first date wearing cutoffs and a tank shirt. He wasn't even wearing slippers. I was relieved when my mother just stared at his bare feet and didn't ask him to wash them before coming in the house.

"I thought you were going to a party," my mother whispered to me in the bedroom.

"We are," I said. "I guess I overdressed." I unzipped my dress as we spoke and yanked a pair of bell-bottoms off a hanger.

"You're not going to wear that!"

"This isn't a prom!"

"I know, but he looks so cheap."

"He's not cheap. His parents have a house near Diamond Head. He lives with them."

"So why doesn't he take you someplace nice? Why does he dress like a bum?"

"Everybody dresses like that. Buzzy wears cutoffs all the time. You just don't like him because he's haole."

"I didn't say that," said my mother. "Your father expects you home by eleven."

"Eleven! You let me stay out as long as I wanted with Weyland Pang."

"Weyland never kept you out all night."

"And Rascal's not going to either!"

"Who?"

"I mean Roger."

"Rascal? Is that his name? I should have known."

"Oh, Ma. That's only a nickname. From when he was a kid."

"He has a double cowlick," said my mother. "I should have known."

"Should have known what?"

"I can tell he's a rascal just by looking at his eyes. You know, the way they sparkle. Like he's up to something."

"Oh, Ma."

"Don't 'Oh, Ma' me. Eleven o'clock. That's it. Or you can forget about going out with him again."

I had expected a reaction, but not a curfew. It was stupid, grossly unfair, not to mention ridiculous. Why did they let me go away to school if they were so worried about me? Why didn't they ask me about what I did or who I dated when I was away? I wrote them letters once a week and occasionally stuck in a male name. They never inquired, never lectured me on how to behave. Couldn't they see how absurd this was? I lay awake at night trying to figure out how I could show them they were wrong about Rascal, wrong about my ability to take care of myself.

———

I turned to Aunty Nona for advice. I figured she, if anybody, would understand.

"How come Popo let you go out with haoles? How come she let you go out with Benny Rapoza?"

"Benny wasn't haole," said my aunty. "Portuguese isn't the same as haole. Besides, all of them were local boys."

"But Rascal is a local boy," I told my aunty. "At least, he is now. I mean, he lives with his parents. It's not like he's a tourist or a service kid."

"They're just worried about you," said Aunty Nona. "They're afraid you'll get in trouble."

"But I could have gotten in trouble with Weyland Pang! I could get into trouble on the mainland! I mean, if Rascal and I are going to do anything, we can do it in broad daylight! Why wait until midnight?"

I knew I'd said too much, but it was too late to retract my words. Besides, Aunty Nona was not just my aunty. She was my friend. We worked together. I expected her to understand.

She said, "Listen, Mahi. Just do what they tell you. If you listen, they'll change their minds."

"How do you know?"

"I just know."

———

I think one of the reasons Aunty Nona was so good at selling seeds was that she knew how to make you want what she wanted to sell. I got hungry just watching her eat. She made everything she ate look so ono. She'd pop a seed into her mouth and roll it around with her tongue. Some people, like me, hold back, take their time, try to make the seed last. I liked to eat li hing mui by pressing it into the center of a half of fresh lemon. Then I'd lick the seed and lemon slowly. A seed could last the whole day like that. Or I'd bite off a bit of seed and let it lie in the hollow of my cheek, not chewing, not swallowing, just letting the little bit of sweet and salty flavor trickle down my throat. After a while I'd have nothing left but the hard seed kernel, which I'd suck until all the flavor was gone. Aunty Nona, on the other hand, would let the seed rest in her mouth for only a few seconds, just long enough to soften it. Then she'd chew and suck noisily, quickly, and the seed would be gone in no time flat.

She laughed at the way I ate. "Why are you saving it?" she'd ask me. "Better eat it fast. Otherwise somebody will eat up the rest."

I hid my bags of seed from Nani and my brothers. I tried to eat fast, like my aunty, but I was always disappointed when I had eaten them all. I wanted the seeds to last forever, but they never did. Even if I could get more, I didn't like facing an empty bag. I wasn't at all like my aunty, who didn't worry about saving seeds for the next person or the next day, who could eat and enjoy, even up until the minute the whole bag of seeds was gone.

For an entire month I pined over Rascal, wishing I could date him more openly, wishing I could be the Mahi who blossomed in Oregon. My friends were right. I was fading, losing my color, but not from the weaker Oregon sun.

My parents didn't come out and say it in so many words, but I knew there was something about Rascal they didn't like. I decided it was because they didn't understand him. He wasn't born in the islands, so they didn't know what his family would be like. They didn't know what to expect, therefore they didn't trust him. He came on pretty strong, after all. Not like the local boys, who tended to play it cool. Who knew how to talk deferentially to my parents. Rascal didn't know any of that. He even tried to sweet-talk my mother! She didn't understand that he was just being nice. That flirting was something that came second nature to him. I knew it wouldn't help to remind them that I could date a lot of Rascals, any Tom, Dick, or Harry Jones, when I was away in Oregon. What amazed me most about the mainland was the realization that I could go for so many miles in one direction before arriving back at home. My choices seemed infinite. Yet my parents kept pulling me back to the finite, back to their narrow, island way of thinking.

When I think back to why I was first attracted to Rascal, I have to search hard for an answer. My feelings about him are so tied up with the way my parents reacted to him at the time. Sometimes I think I liked him because he liked me and wanted to be with me so much. I loved the way his hair wouldn't stay combed, the way it curled after he'd been swimming. He was only slightly taller than me, and strong, but not what you'd call muscular. In fact, he could have used more meat on him, which didn't surprise me when I met his mother.

———

Rascal lived with his mother and stepfather near Diamond Head, close to the lookout point. He invited me to his house on our second date. He said we would have dinner with his parents, then go to a party later. I was thrilled, of course. I figured he must really be serious. None of my dates had ever taken me home to meet his parents, not even Weyland. Even though Rascal showed up in cutoffs again, I kept my red dress on and packed some grubbies to change into later. I imagined a candlelight dinner, with wine, real wine, instead of beer, the whole bit. But instead, the house appeared to be empty when we arrived.

Rascal buzzed the gate so we could get in the driveway. We crossed a stone bridge over a pond to get from the front door to the living room. Carp swam among the water lilies. One wall of the living room was missing, and I found myself gazing out into a courtyard complete with fountains and palms and flowers. When I walked out into the courtyard, I discovered that all the rooms of the house opened onto it. Not sliding doors but whole walls, as if the house were half naked. I could see into all the rooms from where I stood. Even though there was a high wall with barbed wire circling the house, I felt exposed.

"This is incredible," I said to Rascal. "I didn't know people lived like this."

He shrugged, like it was nothing to him. He took my hand and led me to the kitchen.

"Where are your parents?" I asked. I didn't see them, and I didn't smell any food cooking. Maybe we're having salad, I thought.

Rascal didn't answer. He opened the cupboard and took out a can of tuna fish. I noticed that the shelves were almost bare, without cans piled high and threatening to fall out, like in my family's cupboards.

"I thought we were having dinner with your parents," I said.

He shook his head. "My mother has a headache and my stepfather had to work. We'll do it another time. But we can still eat without them, can't we?" He looked up and smiled just a little.

"Sure," I said, leaning into him, hiding my face.

His mother walked into the kitchen just then. I couldn't figure out where she'd come from. I thought I'd seen all the rooms. She wore a bikini. Her skin was baked dark and her stomach was amazingly flat.

"Oh, it's you," she said to Rascal, ignoring me.

"This is Mahi," said Rascal.

"Hello, Mrs. Lang," I said. "I'm so happy to meet you."

"Lacey," she said. I couldn't decide if that was her first or last name. Was she being friendly or reminding me that she was divorced? She gave me a cursory smile, then turned to Rascal and said, "Why don't you fix me a sandwich, sweetie. No mayonnaise." She pecked him on the cheek and left the kitchen.

It occurred to me that maybe she didn't know I was

coming for dinner. That Rascal had hoped for something to happen when he showed up with me. I began to feel sorry for him, although he had a mother who didn't look like a mother, or maybe because he did. I wondered what his parents thought of me, and then it struck me that they probably didn't think about me at all. That Rascal had probably not even told them about me. We sat in the kitchen on high stools and ate our tuna sandwiches in silence.

That night we parked in the cane fields. Since most of the fields were gone, we had to drive pretty far up the hill to find a dirt road. I let him feel how wet my panties were. I let him feel me through my clothes and under. "Mahi, Mahi," he said, running my name together so that it was like the fish, only the way he said it I felt like water spilling out, never to be put back again. I held his head in my lap and stroked his hair and his forehead, as if he were a child with a fever and I was the only one who could take away the heat.

———

Aunty Nona was the one who taught me how to eat crackseed. I mean really eat crackseed, the real kind of crackseed, with the seed inside smashed into many little bits, so you have to be careful how you eat. A really good crackseed eater can separate the bits of seed from the fruit using only the tongue and the teeth, never the hands. You can see the seed flopping around as the lips part slightly, but the seed never touches the fingers again once it enters the mouth. Aunty Nona was so good she could eat crackseed and talk at the same time. My mother was good at it too. She and my aunty could eat crackseed and talk and laugh and continue to do whatever else they were doing with their hands at the time. I could only eat. Very carefully and very slowly, so as not to bite my tongue. Sometimes the whole thing would get out of hand. The seed would open up into one huge blob that evaded my teeth, no matter how quickly I flipped my tongue. When that happened, I'd have to reach in with my fingers and tear off a small chunk and work on just that piece. It was depressing. I'd get so mad at myself. Why couldn't I be like them?

———

Rascal and I talked about prejudice. It was ignorance, of course, that caused people to judge a person by his or her color. Rascal said his parents didn't care whom he married, why should mine? Didn't they see the irony? I had to admit he was right.

"We're the beginning," he said to me. "We shall overcome." It was corny, but I knew he meant it, and I wanted to believe we could make a difference.

We phoned Arlene Murakami and Brian McCloskey, a married couple who wrote a newspaper column for teenagers called "Ask Allie and Bri." Would they give us some advice? They invited us to visit them at home one evening. I had to lie, tell my parents I was going out with the gang. We sat on the floor on tatami mats, and Bri cut the custard pie we'd brought into four equal slices. Allie and Bri told us about how they met at Northwestern, how her parents did not approve of him until they heard him speak Japanese. I loved the way they lived, in a house with shoji sliding doors, the way Bri cut the pie, the way Bri cleared the dishes while Allie showed us clippings from their column about interracial dating and interracial marriage.

Rascal continued to hound me about Maui. "If your brother can do it, so can you." I'd told him about how Buzzy had gone to Maui with a girl when my father got him out of the draft. How I'd envied my brother because he'd done something I could never do.

"Can't you see the double standard?" asked Rascal.

"Sure I can."

"Then do it. Tell them you're going to stay with a friend."

"But what about work? How am I going to get out of that?"

"Tell your aunty. She'll understand. She'll be on our side."

But I wasn't too sure, even if my aunty did remind me of orchids. The orchids my mother grew on the back fence. The orchids I'd seen growing on trees, rather than in pots. My mother explained that that's how orchids used to grow, on trees in the jungle, when the islands used to be jungle. The trees gave the orchids support and protected them from too much light. The orchids thrived on a delicate balance of water and light and air. My mother's orchids grew out of hapu, a native tree fern, bound together with wire, or placed in concrete pots. Unless it rained, my mother watered her orchids every morning and then again at dusk. I was awed by the orchid roots, by the way they grew right through the hapu, out of the holes in the bottoms of the pots, into the air. They needed to breathe.

Aunty Nona was like that. Not caught in the dirt of what people said about her or what they wanted her to be. She needed people, but she didn't like to be root-bound. She needed space. So she walked away when people crowded her too much, and she had a way of making things hers, of making people want what she wanted them to want, and this came to her as naturally as breathing.

———

She knew something was up when I returned to the shop. When a customer asked me a question about one of the seeds, I shrugged instead of giving him a sample. I didn't tell him what I liked about the seed in such a way that he couldn't resist. I had hung around my aunty long enough to know that much. She had to take over, steer him toward the right jar.

"Is it Rascal?" she asked after the customer left.

I nodded. I was afraid to speak, afraid I might cry.

"You're seeing him a lot." She said this matter-of-factly, as if she were describing the color of his hair. I had made up luncheon dates with girl friends, bought clothes on the fly so I'd have something to show her. It was such a relief to be caught.

The words spilled out. "Did you sneak around with Benny Rapoza? I mean, before you were allowed to go out?"

"Sure."

"How come you never married him?"

She didn't answer right away. For a moment I caught a glimpse of the Nona I remembered as a child. She'd gained a lot of weight since then and wore tent dresses instead of sheaths, but I could still picture her. Sassy, winking, making Benny Rapoza's eyes go big.

"I didn't want to," she said.

"But he was crazy about you."

"I know."

"And you begged Popo to let him take you out."

"That's right."

"Then what happened?"

"She finally gave in. She let me go out with him as much as I wanted."

"And?"

"And I found out I didn't love him."

———

I told Rascal Lang I couldn't go to Maui with him. He didn't take it as hard as I thought. Just kept eating his rainbow shave ice and nodding as if he had expected my answer. We were sitting on a bench, sharing a cone. I'd let him pick the flavors. To my surprise, he chose pineapple, which spoiled the vanilla and collided with the root beer. I couldn't eat it, so he took the shave ice from me.

"Let's go out to eat on Saturday," he said. He wanted to take me to the new steakhouse in Waikiki, where his stepfather had already set up an account. "I mean, if you've never eaten Chateaubriand . . ." He smacked his lips.

"I can't," I said.

"What, can't eat Chateaubriand? It's only steak."

"Don't fool around. I mean I can't go out."

"But it's our night to go out," he said. "I'm leaving on Sunday. Your parents have to let you. They promised."

"My family is having a potluck," I said. "It's Aunty Nona's birthday. I have to go." I knew he was waiting for me to invite him. "It's only for family," I lied. His face darkened. "You really don't want to be there," I added.

He didn't hesitate this time. His face went smooth. "Sure," he said, giving me a brief hug, then the boyish grin that I loved. "No problem. We can go out when I come back."

———

Aunty Nona brought her usual baked beans with Portuguese sausage to the potluck. She invited her boss, Sonny Lim, and his wife too. My mother said Nona didn't have to cook anything, seeing as how it was her birthday.

"But everybody likes my beans," said Aunty Nona. "Wouldn't be right."

The uncles usually complained about Aunty Nona's beans. They accused her of being able to cook only that one dish. They said if they farted, it was all her fault. This made me mad, of course. I came to her defense, pointed out all the other gassy foods at the table. I served myself an extra-big helping of my aunty's beans. Her friends took big helpings too, as did Sonny and Eloise Lim on the night of my aunty's birthday. The uncles grumbled about Aunty Nona's friends too. So did the aunties and my parents. Aunty Nona always invited friends to the family parties, often people she barely knew, like the garage mechanic and his wife, grocery-store clerks, friends of friends visiting from the mainland. She loaded up her plate with everyone else's good cooking and made sure her friends got enough to eat too.

"Try these spareribs," she said to the Lims that night. She picked through the dish to find them pieces with lots of meat. "And you have to try the noodles. Anna makes the best gon lo mein."

Aunty Nona's baked beans were delicious. The Portuguese sausage spiced up the beans, and the molasses and honey caramelized into a rich, deep brown sauce. Every spoonful melted sweet and hot on my tongue. I took pleasure in noting that, despite their grumbling, the uncles ate Aunty Nona's beans too. By the end of the potluck, as in every family potluck I had been to, all her beans were gone. Every bean, every sausage, the whole glass dish scraped clean.

Makai

Remember how you learned, when you were a child, how to find where you wanted to go and how to come back home? You learned what all the island people know, about how to go mauka, toward the mountains in the middle of the island, and how to go makai, toward the ocean lying all around. All other directions were marked by places you already knew how to find: Diamond Head, Pearl Harbor, Kaneohe Bay, Waianae.

How easy it was. When we got lost and our friends said, "Just go mauka," we went. When we were hungry, they gave us fish and poi. They invited us to come to their house for kalua pig and lau lau. We could bring our whole family, all our friends. We were never without laughter and love. There were always plenty keiki running around. The uncles played the ukulele and the aunties danced the hula. Do you remember the bass your father, Kuhio, played, with the string tied to the broomstick and stuck in a bucket of sand? We ate and sang the whole night long. We sang and talk story, just like I am now talking to you.

Do you remember the day your mama got lost? She was trying to find my house, here, up in Manoa Valley. I did not want to live makai anymore. Here, I am safe from the tidal wave. Your mama stopped the car to ask an old man the way. Mauka, he said to her. Just go mauka and you run into it. Which way mauka? you shouted out the window. Be quiet, your mama said, but you yelled and cried all the way to my house.

When you reached my house, you ran inside, shouting, Aunty Hannah Mele, Aunty Hannah Mele, which way is mauka, which way is mauka? Your mama thought you were being a smart aleck. She said you always asked too many questions and would not listen to what you were told. Mauka is toward the mountain, I told you. I know that, you said, but the last time we went mauka it was to Uncle You Jook's house on the other side of the island. How can mauka be two different ways? We laughed at you, but you were right. That is how I knew you would be leaving us someday.

How could you stay? The island mauka was not enough. You wouldn't go where the old man sent you. When we went to look at the house where you were born and the stream where the mullet ran and the graveyard where your popo and goong goong were buried, you wanted to know the names of the streets. You wanted to see the lines drawn on the map. What map? Nobody used maps. You were just a girl, but you had one. It was old and torn, but you took it everywhere you went. You were not content to stumble across what you were looking for. When you were only three years old, you told me, Aunty, I am going to find Goong Goong. Which street goes mauka to heaven?

So you see, I was not surprised when you went away, when you went makai and makai and makai, way across the ocean, to the other side. You were looking for something, your own kind of mauka. I saw you go and I waited. I waited for you to come back, to knock on my door and say, Aunty Hannah Mele, let me tell you what I saw.

Now we sit and we talk, you still young and me already old. I planted this banana grove when you were just a baby, and look at it now. I like to sit out here in the shade and feel the cool air. It is still quiet up here, except for the birds so loud in the morning. I hear them when I wake up and I am glad we are both still alive.

We talk about the early days, before the freeway, when our family lived in Waikiki and we never locked our doors. In the summer we slept on the beach at Lanikai and nobody asked us for a camping permit.

Do you remember driving over the old Pali highway, to get to the windward side of the island? Do you remember how the road wound along the cliff and everybody drove so slow? We could not go fast then, not like you can now when you take the freeway through the tunnel. But that was okay. We were not in a rush. We took our sweet time and we always got where we wanted to be.

On the Pali road the wind shook the car, and everybody got scared, except for you. When we stopped to look over the edge, you begged to climb on the rock wall. Your eyes burned like lava, fresh from the volcano. I knew Pele had gone inside your body, and she was talking for you. She was making you brave. I told your mama, Better not make Pele mad, but your mama made you go back inside the car. Sometimes I ask myself, Was it Pele who took you away?

Now you sit close by me and ask me how it was long ago—before Pearl Harbor, before you were born. I tell you about growing taro in the mud. I can still feel the mud on my feet, between my toes. So soft and warm, just like walking on gravy. I tell you about picking opihi on the rocks, how we had to pick fast and then run on the rough coral before the waves washed us off. So many people died that way, but not us kids. We had tough feet, but I tell you, I was always scared. You ask about your goong goong and my kupuna. You ask what it was like when I lived on Maui. But why do you not ask me, Aunty, which way is mauka? Why do you not ask me now, when I am finally ready to tell you?

Let me tell you a story that is mine, that I have never told you before.

I had a baby girl who died. Nobody talks about her anymore, because they do not want to make me sad. She was my second girl. When she was only a month old, she was hanaied, adopted by my family on Maui. I gave her to my parents because they were so lonely for me when I left for Honolulu. Her name was Leialoha. She was the lei of love I gave to my family. When she was only two years old, she died of influenza. She was gone before I could return to see her. In those days we could not fly back and forth between the islands like we can now. My heart was so broken, I did not go home until my papa died. When I finally returned to Maui, I searched for her bones. They said my papa had so much grief he hid her bones in the old Hawaiian style. Nobody knew for sure where he laid her. Some said mauka, up past the waterfalls, above the pools of Kipahulu. Some said more makai, way beyond Kaupo. I did not know how far to go mauka or which way to go makai. I walked up and down the naked side of Haleakala until my feet had blisters. I walked along the ocean, on the lava path of the King's highway, crying "Leialoha, Leialoha," calling for my baby to come back, but the wind and the waves took my voice away.

I still dream about her. I have the same dream again and again. I know in my heart my baby is visiting me, even though she has your face. We are standing on the Pali, and I am holding her hand, only she turns into you, and you want to climb the rock. *This is mauka,* I say. *Where we are now is mauka.* Now let me go, you cry, so I do. I let you go and you jump off the cliff before I can stop you. But instead of falling, you turn into a bird and fly away. You fly makai and makai and makai, until I cannot see you anymore. When I wake up, my face is all wet, not crying wet, but a soft kind of wet all over and through and through. My breasts, my arms, my legs—all wet, as if I have been running through a cloud.

I do not tell you this to make you sad. When I wake up, I do not feel bad. All my pores have been drinking love. It does not matter that I could not find my daughter's bones. She still lives somewhere mauka, where I hold her close, and somewhere makai, where I let her go.

Jade Heart

I saw the light under your bedroom door. All these years, and that's the last thing I see before I go to sleep, the light under your door. Too bad you're not a baby. I could show you the moon and rock you back and forth. Now you are so big, I have to remind myself that you are my baby, I raised you from a pup.

Are you thinking about tomorrow? Still trying to decide what to take? You are worse than me. Don't worry. Just take it all. Uncle Wing can help us with the extra luggage. He knows somebody who can get your bags through.

Maybe you can take this wool coat too. You can wear it on the plane. I'm sure it gets cold in Oregon. I might need it sometime, but I can always borrow it back. In the meantime, you take it. I hate to see it go to waste in the closet.

Let me see you wear it. Oh, you look just like me. No wonder people call us sisters. My hair used to be long like yours, but I wore it pinned up on my head with flowers.

I was so hau po back then. Do you know I bought this coat in San Francisco? It's older than you! So many years ago, but still in fashion. That's why I bought it simple, just a shawl collar, and navy blue is always good, never goes out of style. I wish it was red, but at the time I didn't want to stick out that much. I didn't like when people called me Jap. Makes me sick to my stomach just to think. I had a good time on my own, but sometimes I just wanted to fade away. I wanted to go home. When you wear this coat, I want you to think about how stupid that was. Wasting time being homesick, feeling sorry for myself when I could have been having fun.

Someday maybe, when I come up, we can go to San Francisco. We can dress up and go out to eat. We can ride the trolley to Fisherman's Wharf, just you and me, no uncles or aunties. Nobody telling us what to do. They can drop us off at the bus stop. We can go shopping. I'll show you Chinatown. Where I used to live, if they haven't torn it down.

I'm glad you're going to Oregon. I heard about Oregon when I lived in San Francisco. I hear they have plenty of trees up there. Not as many island people, but just as well. Better if you can get away from so many people telling you what to do. Then you can hear yourself talk. You can hear yourself think.

Sometimes I tell Kuhio, Let's just sell the house and go, but we're still here. I don't know where to go. I can't think of where I want to be. Something inside me just tells me Go, but not all the time. Just when I'm tired. Then I want to go where nobody knows me, where all I have to do is what Anna wants.

I hope you won't be too homesick. Don't worry about

home. I'll write to you and you can write back. I'll send you anything you want. All the food you miss. Seed and mochi crunch. Portuguese sausage. Orchids too.

I'm so jealous. I wish I could be young again and go with you. We could have so much fun. But you can write and tell me. That will be good enough.

Tell me about school, what you are learning. Tell me about your friends, just don't tell me everything. What I don't know won't hurt me. I know you won't do anything bad. I know your father and I brought you up to think for yourself. You're a good girl. When the time comes, you'll know what to do.

Just don't shack up with a man. You might have to get married. Finish school first. Get your degree. These days, it's okay for a girl to be smart. Don't be afraid to speak up in school and let the teacher know you can think. I know you don't always get to say what you want to at home. This is your chance. You can say anything. You can do what you want.

And if it doesn't work out, you still have a home. Don't force yourself to stay away. Nobody's going to take your room. I'll keep your spread on the bed, all of your stuffed animals and books. Everything will still be here when you get back. You don't even have to go, but you know that already. You'll have a good time. I'm so proud of you.

I have only one more thing to give you. Don't worry, it's small. This jade heart. It's from your popo. I was saving it for your thirtieth birthday, Chinese style. But why wait? You might as well wear it now. Going away is just like thirty. You can wear it on the airplane. You can wear it all the time. Popo gave it to me because I was the oldest daughter. Now you are the first, so I give it to you.

Sometimes I think of how much you remind me of your popo. Maybe it is just the way you act. Think how brave she was, coming all the way from China. The only person she knew here was Goong Goong, and then she never went back. She never saw her family again. Lucky thing we have planes. We don't have to say goodbye forever. You can come home anytime.

Don't worry about losing this jade. Just wear it. That's what it's for. When I went to San Francisco, Popo gave me a jade pendant. It was a tear-drop pendant, not a heart. I was only there for one month when I lost it. The clasp on the chain broke. I looked everywhere, at the bus stop, on the sidewalk, in front of my apartment. I was sure I dropped it going to class. I never found that jade. I cried for weeks. I didn't know how I was going to tell my mother. I felt like I had not only lost my jade but my whole family. But when I came home, Popo didn't scold. She just gave me another pendant, this heart, and a new gold chain with a better clasp. She said to me, You have not lost that jade. You will always remember it.

When I was in San Francisco, all I could think about was Hawaii. Now that I am here, I cannot forget San Francisco. I have to remind myself that I have not lost it. It is still there, just like Hawaii will still be here when you are in Oregon. Whatever is lost, you will remember. You will always hold it in your heart.